"Why Did You Come?"

he asked, his voice deceptively silky. "Did you hope that the honeymoon was over and that you could get your foot in the door?"

She stared at him, aghast.

"I warned you. I know everything that goes on on this ranch. You should control your emotions, Jennifer Robins."

Her hand swung, aiming for his face. But he was too quick. Her wrist was caught in a painful grasp.

"No one, I repeat, *no one* ever tries that on me," he said between clenched teeth. "You need a lesson—" He pulled her to him. Before she could protest, his mouth came down on hers. . . .

EDITH ST. GEORGE

is not only an accomplished writer but also a well-known landscape artist. The varied settings of her colorful fiction are as authentic and carefully drawn as her spirited characters.

Dear Reader:

Silhouette Books is pleased to announce the creation of a new line of contemporary romances—*Silhouette Special Editions*. Each month we'll bring you six new love stories written by the best of today's authors—Janet Dailey, Brooke Hastings, Laura Hardy, Sondra Stanford, Linda Shaw, Patti Beckman, and many others.

Silhouette Special Editions are written with American women in mind; they are for readers who want more: more story, more details and descriptions, more realism, and more *romance. Special Editions* are longer than most contemporary romances allowing for a closer look at the relationship between hero and heroine with emphasis on heightened romantic tension and greater sensuous and sensual detail. If you want more from a romance, be sure to look for *Silhouette Special Editions* on sale this February wherever you buy books.

We welcome any suggestions or comments, and I invite you to write us at the address below.

Karen Solem
Editor-in-Chief
Silhouette Books
P.O. Box 769
New York, N. Y. 10019

EDITH ST. GEORGE
Dream Once More

Silhouette *Romance*

Published by Silhouette Books New York

America's Publisher of Contemporary Romance

Other Silhouette Romances by Edith St. George

West of the Moon
Midnight Wine

SILHOUETTE BOOKS, a Simon & Schuster Division of
GULF & WESTERN CORPORATION
1230 Avenue of the Americas, New York, N.Y. 10020

Copyright © 1982 by Edith Delatush

Distributed by Pocket Books

ISBN: 0-671-57126-5

First Silhouette Books printing January, 1982

10 9 8 7 6 5 4 3 2 1

America's Publisher of Contemporary Romance

Printed in the U.S.A.

Chapter One

"Jennifer? I hope I'm not interrupting your writing!"

"Caroline!" Jennie cried, nearly dropping the phone in her surprise. "No, I'm finished. Where are you calling from? You sound like next door.

"Only half a continent away. From the ranch, where else? I thought I'd give you a call since you haven't answered my letter.

"Give me time, it only came a few days ago," Jennie laughed. "I was on the last stretch with my novel and you know how it is. All connections with the outside world are lost until I'm finished."

"Is it done then?"

"Yes. I just sent it to my agent."

"Thank goodness! Now you have no reason not to come for a visit, dear cousin. You're coming to the Dubrow ranch. Fred said to send you a plane ticket so you can't beg off. He knows how much I want to see you."

Jennie couldn't believe it. A six month bride craving company? Then her imagination was not far wrong in sensing a restlessness running through those letters.

"You're tempting me," Jennie admitted. She had seriously considered such a trip but didn't want to intrude on the honeymooners.

"Jennie, please, I need you here. Don't ask questions, just come. Please."

She gave a start. Caroline begging? Her svelte, sophisticated cousin was actually pleading for her to come to the ranch she had raved about in those first letters?

"Is something the matter?" she asked anxiously.

"I'm so glad you can make it, darling. I'll check the airport and send you the ticket for the earliest flight." Her voice had become brightly brittle, one Jennie recognized she had used on irritating customers. Had someone come into the room?

Something *was* wrong and a tingle from apprehension ran down her spine.

"No, wait," she said quickly. "I'll drive out. I always wanted to see the countryside. Who knows, I might pick up background material to use in another novel."

"How soon can I expect you? " The cry was eager.

"Give me a week," Jennie begged, "I have to close the apartment, and it takes a few days to reach you. After all, Chicago isn't next door to Oregon!"

"Oh, Jennie, I can't thank you enough! I'll get the guest room ready. You'll love the ranch. It's your kind of place. Soaring mountains, tremendous space. But I warn you, sheep aren't the dear things you count to go to sleep. Though the lambs are cute . . . " Her voice trailed off wistfully. Again that troublesome undertone.

Jennie sat in the chair a long time after replacing the receiver, recalling the events leading to the phone call.

Two years ago Caroline had coaxed her out of her barely adequate apartment into a joint partnership in this place.

"Look at the possibilities!" she had cried with enthusiasm over the old but large high-ceilinged rooms. "We can breathe here. I can take the bus to work, and you can have the bedroom with the dressing room to use as your workroom. I promise I'll never interfere when you are there chasing your muse."

Jennie had hesitated. "I don't know if I can afford it. I've only sold one novel, and maybe that's all I have in me.

Caroline hooted. "We grew up together, remember? And I'll never forget the stories you always were able to weave whenever we were bored. I never doubted you'd make a success as a writer. My only surprise is you waited so long to start putting them on paper. I knew you wouldn't be happy long as a secretary."

Jennie nodded agreement. Her mother had been firm about choosing a more substantial vocation than the nebulous one of a writer. Only upon her death, and with the security of a modest inheritance to back her, did she dare give up her job and follow her heart's inclination.

The two cousins were remarkably alike, both average height and built along the same slim lines so their wardrobes were interchangeable.

Caroline was a buyer of women's apparel for a fashionable department store downtown in Chicago. She was twenty-three, a year younger than her cousin, but her sophistication, nurtured by her job, made her appear older. Her dark hair was cut cap close and fashionably streaked, but Jennie preferred hers flowing straight to her shoulers. Her eyes were blue to Jennie's gray but otherwise they could pass as sisters.

Everything worked out well for them. Caroline's flair for color changed the apartment into a striking yet warm place.

Jennie typed at her desk and lived through three novels, while Caroline built dreams of opening her own dress shop.

Then one night after a party Caroline brought Fred Dubrow home. Tall, bronzed, *immense*. He filled the apartment, breathing of the great outdoors. His laugh boomed, his eyes crinkled, his mouth lifted easy in a wide smile. His brown eyes never left Caroline.

He was a sheep rancher and he carried the assurance of one who dealt with vast spaces. Jennie could understand her cousin's instant capitulation.

It had been a whirlwind romance. Two weeks. Jennie stood beside the ecstatic bride when the ring was placed on her finger in the Justice of the Peace's office.

"It will be a short honeymoon," Fred had apologized, his big hand amazingly gentle on her cheek. "My brother Wyatt needs help. When I called to tell him the good news, he mentioned there's an increase in rustling again. Also, the lambs will be dropping soon and all hands are needed at home. I'll make it up to you later."

Caroline could only agree, her eyes shining with her love.

The apartment was suddenly empty. Jennie had not realized how the excitement of the two had taken hold. How wonderful it must be to be so in love!

Caroline was a sporadic writer. At first her description of married life on a ranch was almost embarrassingly blissful. Lately Jennie was uncomfortably conscious of an undercurrent of unrest. Was the honeymoon over so soon? She hoped not. They had been so wonderfully in love.

Jennie gave a little sigh as she packed. Soon she'd see what had happened to Caroline's Eden.

"Is the Dubrow Ranch near here?" Jennie asked the attendant as he filled her gas tank.

His eyebrows rose. "Near the Dubrow Ranch?" he mocked. "Lady, you're on, in, surrounded by it."

"If you could give me directions . . . ?"

He waved his hand airily and she realized his act was for his grinning friends sitting in the shade of the storefront.

"From this one, all roads going north lead eventually to the homestead. Pick one that looks the easiest," he answered flippantly.

She soon understood what he meant. Miles of wire fencing threaded alongside the road to be interspaced with an occasional access point. Tall poles with a sign hanging on the crossbar claimed ownership by the Dubrow Ranch. Goodness, how large was the spread!

After passing two gates guarding mere trails, she decided to accept the challenge of the third. She opened it, crossed the iron cattle grill, then dutifully closed the gate behind her.

Jennie had taken her time coming across the plains and the Rockies. This was a new experience. One could read about it but being in it was mind-expanding.

Her city eyes were bedazzled by the im-

mense expanse of the country. No wonder
Fred had filled the apartment. He was part of
this vast land she had barely known existed.

She had picked up Interstate 95 into Oregon
and swept past ancient lava flows and near
deserts. Riverbeds were mere trickles or dry
this late into fall. Because the melting snows
from the mountains had finished their offer-
ings they would remain so until the new build-
up over the winter before becoming roaring
torrents again from the spring runoff.

How could a ranch exist in this setting? She
never realized the barrenness of the south-
eastern part of the state.

She had turned onto the county road until
reaching the town which had been Caroline's
address. Town? All she had seen were the
dual gas tanks in front of the general store/
post office combination.

The land was now mostly sagebrush and
seared grasses, all bleakly barren to her uned-
ucated eyes. There had been scattered clumps
of sheep behind the two wire fences and now
she was driving through them.

The road soon became little more than twin
ruts, certainly not made for her packed mini-
car. A jeep would have a difficult enough
time. She had unkind thoughts for the uncar-
ing boy at the gas pump with his vague in-
structions. Surely there must be a main road
to the house. This was only a feeder route.

The bottom of the car bumped hard against

an exposed rock, causing her to wince. Better be safe and turn around, but how? A mountain loomed ahead and the land on both sides convoluted into rough hills. She was trapped in her narrow lane.

Suddenly to her left she spied a man on a horse topping the incline. The horse tossed its head in rebellion as he began cantering down the slope. It was fighting, showing a will of its own, and she eyed the man pitting his strength against the animal.

Peering ahead, she started down the sharp grade. Perhaps at the bottom there would be a flat area to turn around and the man could direct her to the correct entrance.

The car was gathering speed and she applied the brake. Nothing! There was no response. Something must have broken during that last bump.

Frantic, she pulled at the hand brake. The car slowed for a few minutes but that soon lost its hold.

She was now fighting the wheel, trying to keep it from jumping from her hands when hitting the potholes.

The horse was coming at an angle and they would soon meet. Didn't that man see her? He was bending over the animal's neck talking to it.

Her hand hit the horn button to warn him of the impending danger. The strident blare filled the air and the horse reacted in alarm, rearing with a sharp whinny.

He was off like a shot coming straight for her, and she gasped in horror, knowing she was powerless to avert the collision.

In one powerful surge the horse leaped the road, a hairbreadth in front of her, then galloped on. The muscles on the man's arms were ridges as he fought for control and she caught the swift glare of his fury before they disappeared over the hill.

They were out of her mind just as rapidly. The bottom of the incline was fast approaching and her arms ached as she, too, fought for control.

The car lurched across the small opening but its momentum carried her partly up the next hill before finally halting, nudging precariously against an enormous boulder.

Perspiration covered her face and it took several seconds before she could unclasp her grip on the steering wheel. She leaned against the headrest, completely drained, incapacitated by her ordeal.

Slowly her eyes unglazed and she examained the extent of her predicament. The car was useless to get her out and she was miles from the town. It was getting late. She had discovered dusk came quickly here, bringing cold winds down from the mountains.

Common sense told her to stay in the protection of her car and she fought the urge to run. To one used to bright lights of a large city, the thought of spending a night in the inky blackness of the near desert was terrifying. What kind of animals prowled these lonely stretches?

She shifted uneasily on the seat. That rider. There had been something about him. She had only a quick glimpse of the angry man, but he had looked strangely familiar.

An anger rose in her. Why hadn't the fool man stopped to help her? Couldn't he see she was in trouble? Besides what was he doing riding in this godforsaken land on an unbroken horse!

The sound drifted to her, breaking the unearthly quiet, and she jumped out of the car.

Could help be coming? Yes! The half-truck came over the rise and barreled along the trail to stop behind her.

She stared at the grinning man, then ran to his arms as he jumped down from the cab.

"Hey, there, no need to cry," Fred said, patting her shoulder. "Are you all right?"

All right? She had miraculously averted serious injury, done untold damage to her car and been terrified by the threatening blackness descending on this inhospitable land. And he wondered if she was all right!

Chapter Two

"How did you know I was here?" she asked as he piled her luggage in the back of the truck.

"Wyatt figured it must be you," He explained. "You look enough like Cary to be sisters, you know."

Her anger flared again. "Then it was your brother. Why didn't he stop if he knew it was me?"

"He couldn't figure what you were doing on this track. And as far as stopping, he's shooting lightning bolts over you sounding your horn and spooking Devil."

"He wasn't paying any attention and was coming right at me," she exploded. "Too bad he had such poor control over the horse."

He gaped at her, then let out a roar of laughter. "No control! My god, I'd be unseated and limping home! That horse has defeated us all. This was the first run under a saddle. Evidently he was doing well until your horn spooked him and he took the bit."

She couldn't feel contrite over any discomfort she might have caused that man. Her problems had been as great as his at the time.

"We'll get a chain on your car tomorrow and see what damage has been done. What made you race down the hill?"

"Race! You don't think I was enjoying bouncing down that wretched road without brakes!"

He stared at her, his face paling. "You mean you came down that hill with no brakes?" He gazed back over the incline. "You're one lucky lady!"

He helped her onto the high seat and wrestled the truck along the road to where another rutted lane crossed. This led them onto what was evidently the main drive to the house.

Talk was limited. Fred concentrated on his driving and she on staying in the seat while wondering how many bruises she was accumulating.

He stopped as they topped a slight rise and she took in the scattered grouping of buildings nestled in a small valley. The hills rolled one after the other until stopped by the dark mountains.

"Home," he said, waving his hand, and she concentrated on the sprawling house. The central section was two stories high with a wide porch across its front. Angled single storied wings extended off each side. A stream ran a few hundred feet to one side.

It appeared lushly green after the dried barrenness of the land she had been traveling through. Not until later did she see the intricate irrigation network they had built to create this lovely oasis.

Now it looked like the Eden Caroline had described, serenely quiet.

"Where's Caroline?" she asked, suddenly aware she hadn't been mentioned.

His mouth tightened for a second and his hand went through his thick brown hair.

"She flew into Boise for a few things she said we needed for your visit. I'm picking her up in the morning.

Was there a note of strain in his voice?

"She'll be sorry she gauged your travel time so poorly. We did not expect you until the weekend."

A cold draft reached her. She had an uncomfortable feeling he wasn't overjoyed with her early arrival. Still, he had been warmly solicitous during her exhibition of tears.

"I'm sorry," she said in a small voice. "If you'd rather I wait until Caroline arrives, I'll go to a hotel."

He looked at her in surprise. "What, and have the Dubrow hospitality questioned?"

The remembered grin covered his face as a large hand patted her knee. "Your room is all ready for you, pet. We just won't have the big dinner all set up as planned, but the welcome will be there!"

"Not by your brother," she murmured prophetically.

He heard her and let out his booming laugh. "Wyatt is in for a big surprise. Be easy on him, city girl. He's a hard man, but a good and just one. The rest of us could be more like him."

Jennie stared at him questioningly. As far as she was concerned, all should look up to him.

"Ruth and Dave are anxious to meet you," he continued. "She's feeling better and will be up so you won't be overwhelmed by the Dubrow men."

Jennie suddenly recalled Caroline mentioning the other brother David and his wife Ruth. They had two-year-old twins and Ruth was having another baby. Only this pregnancy had gotten off to a rocky start. She had been confined to her bed for several weeks. It seemed as though her cousin was living in a complicated household. That sprawling house was large but could it manage so many families under one roof? There were indeed thorns in this Eden.

The truck pulled in front of the house and a man and woman came out on the porch. He was a Dubrow, Jennie saw immediately, but not the angry man on the horse.

Dave looked like Fred; two years younger, the edges were a little softened. He came down the two steps in one easy stride his hand outstretched, the same grin on his face, wide and welcoming.

Ruth was softly rounded, with an Irish face sprinkled with freckles. She followed more slowly, cautious after her stay in bed.

"Fred was right," she smiled, giving Jennie a warm hug. "You look enough like Cary to be her sister."

"Our relationship confuses people since we had the same last name," Jennie admitted. "Our fathers were brothers."

She was swept into the house, the men following with the suitcases. The wide porch was screened, and she could see by the well-worn furniture that warm evenings were spent there.

The living room was just as comfortable, though the easy chairs showed the abuse from large bodies dropping into them.

"After our dusty roads, you must be dying for a shower," Ruth said, ordering Fred to show her the bedroom. "Forgive me for not taking you but the doctor warned me against stairs."

Jennie followed Fred back to the entrance hall where sturdy stairs led to the second floor. Upstairs there were three doors. Fred opened one and deposited the cases at the foot of the bed.

"How lovely!" Jennie exclaimed. The ceiling slanted at the far wall but there were wide gables with open windows letting in the last of the afternoon sunshine.

The rough walls were painted white. A heavy woven white spread was on the maple bed and a colorful braided rug covered the floor. The curtains were bright with garden flowers. It was a cheerful country bedroom.

"There's only one bathroom up here," he apologized. "It's an old house and dad put one in when he inherited it from grandpop. There's one downstairs also and in each of the wings," he added hurriedly as if wondering what her city breeding expected in the way of conveniences.

"Which bedroom is yours and Caroline's?" she asked.

"We're not in the main house, didn't Cary tell you? We have the east wing and Dave and Ruth the west. There are two bedrooms and a sitting room in each. We all eat together and usually end up in the big living room downstairs.

"Wyatt's room is next door," he paused, shifting as if embarrassed.

Jennie looked up at him sharply. *Was she to sleep alone on this floor with his miserable older brother?* Her indignation brought a flush.

"We do have two bedrooms," Fred continued uncomfortably, "but I've been using one as a sort of workroom. Wyatt insisted Cary open one of these rooms for you. The other is filled with massive furniture from the grandparents so Cary decided this one was more appropriate."

He cleared his throat. "Look, Jennie, if you prefer being in our wing, I'll haul out my junk."

"If your brother can tolerate my intrusion," she said stiffly, "I'm certain I can bear up also. I promise not to hang my stockings in the bathroom."

He checked for towels on the rack behind the door and informed her dinner was served at seven.

So, she thought, unpacking her clothes, she was isolated here with the older brother who, she was beginning to suspect, held the dominant position in the household.

Sections of Caroline's letters came to mind. At first she had spoken highly about Wyatt but lately there had been an underlying irritation whenever he was mentioned.

Well, Wyatt Dubrow, I shall be on guard about you. Caroline is disenchanted with you and I've seen nothing to impress me so far.

But she was careful to clean the tub and wipe the steam from the mirror when she finished her bath. He wasn't going to find any reason to further vent his spleen on her.

She rested for half an hour. The emotional

excitement of that last hair-raising ride down the steep hill had strained her nerves already tired from the long push across the states.

Jennie dressed for dinner in a warm ivory wool skirt and matching cashmere sweater set. As a buyer, Caroline had bought most of her clothes, picking up tremendous bargains. This outfit, accented by gold jewelry was one of her better finds. Jennie applied makeup lightly, recalling Ruth's scrubbed wholesomeness. Satisfied with the finished result, she stepped into the hall.

The door next to her opened at the same moment, and she looked up to meet the frozen stare of Wyatt Dubrow. His broad frame filled the threshold as he stood there, his eyes moving slowly, insolently, down to her shoes and back up.

"We meet again, Miss Robbins," he said finally, no welcome evident in the cold tone.

Stunned by what felt like a physical impact, Jennie could only nod.

He stepped aside, releasing her from the hypnotic hold of his eyes. He indicated the stairs and she stumbled as she moved toward them. His hand went to her elbow as he guided her down the stairs.

Guided was right. Her mind was scrambling from shock, unable to remember the simple layout of the house. What right had he to glare at her so accusingly? Was he still blaming her because his horse bolted?

A tall, thin, older woman stood in the doorway to the dining room. Her dark blond hair was pulled into a tight knot at the back of her head. Her thin face had a freshly scrubbed look.

"Good evening, Grace," Wyatt said. "Have you met Caroline's cousin Jennifer Robbins? Our cousin, Grace, Miss Robbins."

"I've been busy in the kitchen," she said with a tight smile. Where was this western hospitality Jennie had read about?

The family had already gathered. Fred jumped up to take her hand and lead her into the room. He pressed a drink into her hand and she smiled warmly at him. At least here she knew she had a friend!

The martini was dry as she liked it. He had remembered her preference from Chicago. That little bit of attention eased her tension.

She glanced across the room to be flattened again by the cold cat eyes narrowed in censure. Now, what had she done? Couldn't she even smile at his brother?

She sank into a chair next to Fred. Who cared what his tempermental brother thought? It had nothing to do with her. Nothing whatsoever. It was only too bad that Caroline had to live with such a difficult brother-in-law.

"Cary will be beside herself for not being here to greet you," Ruth said, coming to sit comfortably by her husband.

"I'm sorry to have descended like this," Jennie apologized. "Neither of us mentioned a definite date though I said in about a week. I did want to take the time to investigate sections which looked interesting."

"Yes, Cary said you hoped to find some background material. We read your mysteries, Jennie, and think they're terrific. Is the latest along the same lines?"

"My publisher said to stay with a winning combination."

Wyatt lit a cigarette and squinted through the smoke. "Then you should be able to grind them out as long as you wish."

Jennie flushed at the derision heavy in his voice. "Yes, that is true," she said defiantly. "Just like Gardner, Maclean or Hamilton to mention a few, though I'm not in their league."

"Very modest of you," he said coolly.

"Oh, come on, Wyatt," Fred said into the embarrassed silence. "Pay no attention to Big Brother, Jennie. We're all mystery buffs and have given your novels four stars."

Ruth and Dave were looking at Wyatt with open amazement over the hostile overtones.

Grace appeared announcing dinner and they rose quickly grateful for the interruption.

The three Dubrow brothers stood together for a minute and Jennie realized with surprise they weren't tall men. All were under six feet, but the wide shoulders, the vitality emanating from them, filled the room. They were part of this vast space they moved through out-of-doors, and they carried the aura with them.

She had been acutely conscious of it when Caroline had first brought Fred to the apartment. Dave had it, softened a little, gentled by a loving wife. But in Wyatt! Her nerves tingled with animosity. In him it was magnified to the nth degree. He stood there overwhelmingly domineering, uncomfortably insolent, overbearingly arrogant. Her only desire was to cut him down to size.

It would be impossible, of course, and she turned gratefully to Fred when he came and took her arm to lead her to the dining room. At least with him she could act normal.

The yellow eyes were heavy on her again, and she found herself uncomfortable even while fuming over letting his censure dictate to her.

The meal was a catastrophe. Jennie, who enjoyed creating gourmet meals only next to her writing, was appalled at the food lined on the table.

The leg of lamb was shrunken on the bone, leather hard, the gravy, a pale gelatinous pudding. The canned beans sat sullenly in their juice and the mashed potatoes were mounded, hard lumps.

She saw the silent sigh of resignation Wyatt gave before carving the ruined roast. The men ate doggedly. They worked hard and needed the calories, but Ruth nibbled around the edges, filling up on the rolls. Jennie sat next to her, having carefully chosen the seat farthest away from Wyatt.

The coffee was surprisingly excellent, and she discovered Ruth made it. The Overlord must have insisted on that at least!

Ruth started to clear the table, but Wyatt ordered her to return to the living room.

"Doctor's orders," she sighed apologetically.

"Let me," Jennie offered. "I need some exercise after sitting in the car so much the past few days."

She hurried the cleaning under Grace's watchful eye. She tried to carry on a conversation but Grace did not appear to be the chatty type.

That she could understand. It was Big Brother Wyatt's attitude which confused and angered her. Surely he wasn't still holding the incident with the horse against her. By now he must have found out why she had been speeding down the hill unable to avoid the near accident.

"How do you get your ideas for your novels?" Ruth asked Jennie when Jennie returned to the living room to join the family.

Jennie raised her hands in a helpless gesture. She had heard the question many times. "I don't know. They just come. A chance word or overheard conversation, a small article in the paper. Something happens, ideas fly, and I'm at the typewriter caught up in another story."

Her face was alight with remembered discovery. "It's quite awesome at times. Frequently the characters take over and tell me what happens next. If I fight, they die on me. Then I go for a walk and come back, resigned to letting them have their own way, and it all comes out much better than my original idea."

"I can imagine the work involved," Dave said. "Term papers were enough of a headache."

Jennie nodded. "It can be. I put in long hours. Some days the pages fill in a hurry. Other times I'm lucky to do two or three. But I do it every day for weeks at a time until it's finished. Caroline will tell you I literally go into hibernation."

"It's not as easy as one thinks," Fred said, coming to sit by her. "Have you another plot ready?"

"Oh, yes. But I refuse to start it until I'm back in Chicago, or you won't see me. I'd be closeted in my room all the time. Writing is a jealous mistress. It demands all of one's attention."

"We'll have to make arrangements to haul Jennie's car tomorrow," Fred said, abruptly changing the subject. "I hope the brakes can be fixed."

Wyatt raised an eyebrow. "Brakes?" he repeated.

"Yes. She must have bottomed on a rock and ruptured the fluid line. That's why she was tearing down that hill when you were out on Devil."

"Did you think I always drove like that?" Jennie's voice was saccharine sweet, but she let him see the scorn in her eyes.

"I was not exactly in a position to tell, Miss Robbins," he answered. "Did you think you were riding the Loop in Chicago, blaring your horn? Devil was skittish enough without adding that noise to make him bolt."

"I assure you I had your best interests at heart, Mr. Dubrow. We were on a collision course. I saw you leaning over your horse and was afraid you hadn't seen me. At that point I knew I had little control over my car."

"I was well aware you were there, Miss Robbins," he answered, his voice several degrees colder. "You will find I always know what's happening on the ranch. Even when some fool attempts to drive a mini-car on a feeder road."

Jennie flushed, even as her tone iced to match his. "Then you better instruct the attendant at the local station, Mr. Dubrow. He informed me I could take any road in. He assured me they all led to the house."

He raised an eyebrow in disbelief. "Come now, you could see the condition of the road, Miss Robbins. Even one city bred would know they were only used to reach the sheep."

Her eyebrow raised in equal disdain. "How was I to know that wasn't the condition of all your driveways, Mr. Dubrow?"

Fred's deep chuckle broke in. "Give it to him, Jennie! I do believe Lord Wyatt has met his match!"

"Honestly now," Ruth chided. "Where did all the formality come from?"

"Did you really lose your brakes?" Dave asked anxiously. "You did a neat bit of driving then if you controlled it down that steep slope."

Jennie tossed a triumphant glance at the older brother, but his face was stonily impassive.

"It was nerve-racking," she admitted. "I hope I never have to go through it again." She could sense Wyatt's eyes on her.

Conversation lagged. The morning's work started at daybreak and the men were tired.

"I'll be going to town early for Cary. Want to come along, Jennie?" Fred asked.

"I'd love to but I'm bushed. I have no idea

29

when I'll wake up. I'll wait here if that's all right," she answered.

"Fine," he agreed with a smile. "It will give her time to blow off steam over missing you.

Then, I'll say good-night. Hope you sleep well in the new bed."

Jennie gave her wide smile. He was as big-brotherly as she remembered.

"Nothing will keep me awake," she assured him.

He strode to the door that led to his wing of the house, and Jennie moved to the stairs.

Upstairs, through the window at the end of the hall, the moon made a bright patch on the carpet. She went to gaze outside and caught her breath at the beauty of the silvery landscape. The undulating hills gave way to a soaring mountain, all dramatically highlighted and accented by dark shadows.

"You should see it outside to get the full effect."

Startled, she looked at the man standing next to her. He moved silently for so large a person.

"It's magnificent from here," she said, eyeing him warily.

Wyatt stared broodingly out the window and she studied him for the first time. The features which were slightly blurred in Dave, and more clearly outlined in Fred, were sharply delineated in this man. His nose was more angled, his jaw line leaner. He didn't have cat's eyes, she decided. Yellow, yes, but they were the eyes of a hawk. God help any prey if he decided to pounce!

"Come with me," he ordered. "Put on something warm. It gets cold at night now."

She started to decline, then hesitated. Was he offering her an olive branch? It would be more gracious to accept.

The cold air hit her as they went silently outside. She hurriedly pulled the zipper on her quilted jacket. Heavens, it wasn't winter as yet. What would it be like when the temperature really dipped!

The ground crunched underfoot as they walked around the house until they had the same view as from the window above.

The velvet sky studded by bright stars was dominated by a three-quarter moon. The mountain rose majestically. Silver highlights with contrasting black shadows created a sur-realistic painting, awe-inspiring in the vast-ness of the canvas. An intense yearning rose in her. Her arms rose as if needing to physi-cally clasp the view in a close embrace. They then dropped helplessly to her side. The beauty caught at her heart and she fought a sudden desire to cry.

Nothing had ever affected her so pro-foundly, and she turned to the silent man, eyes wide with wonder, to find him staring down at her.

31

"There are no words, are there," she whispered, not wanting to intrude into the intense silence.

"Competes with skyscrapers?" he questioned.

She gave an impatient shrug. There was no comparison and well he knew.

"I never professed to be in love with Chicago. That was where Caroline's work was and we shared an apartment."

"Did you know Fred before Caroline did?"

She looked at him warily. What was he leading up to? "No. She met him at a party. I was introduced when he brought her home. It was a storybook romance. Love at first sight, and wedding bells in two weeks."

"In stories they live happily ever after," he said.

"Yes," she answered, instantly alert. Did he also suspect something was wrong between them?

"Why did you come?" he asked, his voice deceptively silky. "Did you hope the honeymoon was over and you could get your foot in the door?"

She stared at him aghast, too shocked to feel anger.

"I warned you I knew everything that happened on the ranch," he said harshly. "That means the people on it, also. You should control your emotions more, Jennifer Robbins, watch that special smile for Fred. His wife might be having a little difficulty adjusting, but I assure you I will let nothing nor anyone disrupt the lives of my family. Not even a lovesick cousin who Cary inadvertently trusts."

Jennie never let her heroines react this way. It was archaic and overused, but her hand swung, aimed for his face.

He was too quick. Her wrist was caught in a painful grasp.

"No one, I repeat, no one, ever tries that on me," he said through clenched teeth.

She was pulled roughly against him. "You need a little lesson, spitfire."

His mouth came down on hers in a cruel meeting of lips. His arms were steel bands denying escape or movement.

Her senses were in shock as she struggled fruitlessly.

Slowly, with knowing expertise, he raped her mouth until he effectively tore all resistance to shreds. Her arms possessed a will of their own as they crept around his neck, her body moved to mold tightly against his while she answered him with an abandonment never before aroused.

Finally, when the world was ready to explode, taking her with it, he lifted his head.

She stared at him dazedly, craving his lips again no matter how painful it was.

His chest expanded as he drew in a sharp breath, then his hands closed over her wrists, releasing their hold around his neck.

"So, little cousin, is that how you were going to lure Fred?"

The icy words pounded down, stunning her. A cry of pain escaped and she stumbled away from him to run to the house.

Chapter Three

Jennie slept late, but only because she had tossed restlessly until the sky began lighting in its predawn gray.

She crept downstairs, hoping the men were off doing chores. Fred would be going for his wife, and she struggled to pull herself together before Caroline's arrival. Could she blame the shadows under her eyes on exhaustion from the trip?

Everyone would accept that explanation. Everyone except one damnable man she already hated with a passion. Why had she ever come!

Ruth eyed her when she came down. "Difficult sleeping in a new bed?"

Jennie forced a light laugh. "A little. It was comfortable enough, but I was still driving the car. I'll be relaxed enough tonight to make up for it."

"Just made a fresh pot of coffee," Ruth said. "Grace is keeping an eye on the twins for me. Come. I'll make your breakfast."

The eggs were poached just right, and Jennie indulged in two muffins.

"Is Grace a real cousin?" she asked. The title was often given to a close friend.

"Yes," Ruth said. "Several times removed, but the relationship is there. That's why when Wyatt found she had nowhere to go after her last job, he offered her a place here. I had the twins and he thought she could help. Besides, he only acted true to form. He loves acting the patriarch and has to keep an eye on the family."

Jennie shivered, remembering his words of warning the night before. Oh yes! He took care of his family all right!

"When is your baby due?" Jennie asked, refilling their coffee cups.

"In four months."

"Twins expected again?"

"Heavens, no! We'd bulge out of our suite if that happened. As it is we've changed the sitting room into our bedroom so we'd have a place for the baby."

Jennie recalled Fred's description of the wings. Two bedrooms, a sitting room and bath, he had said.

"I better go check on the twins," Ruth said. "Leave the dishes. Grace will do them."

"It will only take a minute," Jennie protested. "I'll come out to join you as soon as I'm finished."

"I warn you, come at your own risk. They'll

wear you out in no time!" Smiling indulgently, Ruth walked out.

Grace came in for her coffee break. Jennie gave her a welcoming smile.

"Ruth was just telling me she didn't know how she would have coped without your help," she started cheerfully. She draped the towels to dry and continued, "I hope I am putting things in the right place. I know how irritating it can be to reach for something and find it isn't there."

She had almost reached the door when she heard Grace chuckle and remark, "The moonlight is pretty here, isn't it?"

Jennie hurried outside, her cheeks flushed. Well! Grace might be shy but when she decided to talk, she dropped her bombs!

Only then she realized the woman's bedroom was in the back of the kitchen. She had a front row seat last night when Wyatt held her bound to him, expertly feeding the fire he had started.

Darn the man! Even the memory could start her trembling. He had to be carefully avoided in the future.

She found Ruth in the play yard off her wing. Rachel and Rudy were bewitching children, happy to discover a new playmate.

Once she knew the children accepted her, she made Ruth go in to rest. The doctor had let her out of bed on trial, and Jennie could see her wilting.

The children were soon industriously assisting her build castles in the sandbox when Wyatt found them there. She was laughing with the squealing children over a toppled castle, and she glanced up to see him leaning against a tree, squinting at them through a curl of cigarette smoke.

"Uncle Wy!" they shouted gleefully, running to him.

He hunched down, and a child ran into each arm, to be lifted and swung around.

He finally deposited them on the ground and they noisily informed him how they were helping Auntie Jen.

"Where's Ruth?" he asked over their chatter.

"I told her to rest," she answered, keeping her face averted.

She had watched unbelieving as he had laughed with the children. Was this the same man who had crucified her last night?

"So now I have to watch out for Dave, also," he murmured.

"Darn you!" she flared, furious. "Get off my back! You're completely detestable. As soon as I see Caroline I shall leave since you seem to think my presence is more than the Dubrow men can handle. I, for one, have had enough of the Mighty Wyatt. You're contemptible and obnoxious, and I hope I never have the misfortune to see you again!"

The children were silent, their mouths turning down in reaction to the sharp words.

"Oh, go away," she cried, struggling to keep her voice from breaking. Picking up a toy shovel with a trembling hand, she lashed furiously at a castle, causing it to fall. The children laughed and helped demolish the rest. When she finally looked up again, he was nowhere in sight.

The pickup truck lumbered by, her car in tow. Taking the children by hand, she followed it to the barn.

Dave was there talking to a man already under the car.

"Ruptured the line as we thought, and lost the brake fluid," he informed her. "We'll have to order the part."

"Will it take long?" she asked, the distress evident in her voice. "I had planned to go on to see the Pacific after the visit with Caroline. My time is limited."

"Why the rush?" he asked in surprise. "You don't have a boss you have to report back to."

No, but there was a boss here whom she wanted to run from, she thought bitterly.

"Besides, I for one would like to know you better," he continued. "Cary has had nothing but glowing words about you."

Wyatt wheeled out from under her car, and

Dave's fateful words echoed in her ears. She met the cold glitter in Wyatt's eyes and her heart sank. He was twisting those words, giving them the worst possible interpretation.

She gave Dave a weak smile and hurried the children back to the play yard.

For Pete's sake, she muttered with irritation. That man is driving me crazy.

"Jennie! There you are! How good to see you again." Caroline came flying out of the house, and the cousins hugged each other happily.

"Don't tell me they have you baby-sitting already," Caroline laughed, unashamedly wiping at her tears.

"I'm giving Ruth a chance to rest. I've been reintroduced to the glories of the sandbox," she grinned, then looked critically at the girl in front of her.

"You've lost weight. I thought marriage was supposed to have the opposite effect?"

Caroline gave a wry smile and raised her hand in a weary gesture. Immediately Jennie's suspicions zeroed on Wyatt. What had that despicable man done to rock her marriage? They had left Chicago glowingly in love. The restless note had only crept into her letters the past two months, and she held no doubt that Big Brother had something to do with it. Look what he had done to her in less than twenty-four hours.

"Fred told me about the harrowing experience you had yesterday. He stopped and gave

Jack at the gas station a good talking to. The stupid kid!"

"I should have suspected something when I saw his friends giggling," Jennie admitted. "He had me pegged right as an easy mark, fresh from the city. I'm afraid your brother-in-law will never forgive me for frightening his horse that way."

"Wyatt?" she said in surprise. "I wouldn't worry about him. Once he understood the circumstances, all would be forgiven. Besides you are family so you can do no wrong."

How little she knew! The only kindness Wyatt had shown Jennie was during those few minutes when they had shared that breath-taking moonlight scene. And even that was marred. He had used the invitationas an excuse to brutally condemn her.

Ruth had evidently fallen asleep so they each took a child and led them in for lunch.

The men came in shortly and Fred bent over his wife to place a kiss on the nape of her neck.

"Careful," Caroline laughed up at him. "You'll be getting applesauce all over you. I swear I'm swimming in it."

"You faring any better?" he asked, roughing Jennie's hair.

Careful, she warned herself. Big Brother is watching to see your reaction.

"Not much," she admitted lightly. "I'm not

worrying. It must be good for the complexion. Look at theirs."

"Skin like yours needs no aid," Dave said gallantly, then looked around anxiously. "Where's Ruth, is she all right?"

"She's fine," Caroline said reassuringly. "Jennie did her good deed for the day and baby-sat, letting her nap."

"What do you think of my cousin, Wyatt?" she asked as he leafed through the mail. "Pretty as I told you?"

He looked up and his yellow eyes swept coolly over Jennie. "If not watched, she could become the *femme fatale*," he warned.

Jennie gritted her teeth, denying the acid return she longed to fling at him. She turned her back to him, not giving him the satisfaction of seeing her having to swallow her temper.

The men were soon deep into ranch talk and Jennie found it fascinating listening. It ranged from a new tick dip to market prices and on to the rustling discovered too late on one of the ranches. Seeing her cousin's obvious boredom, Jennie's worry deepened.

When they left to check a fence line, Jennie went with Caroline to her wing of the house.

"You haven't lost your flair!" she enthused, admiring the decor.

Caroline had brought in the blues of the changing sky and the rich browns and greens of the land. Bright splashes of yellow and orange spiced the earth tones.

"What do your friends think of it?" Jennie asked.

Caroline gave the weary shrug Jennie had noticed and worried over. "Somehow when I invite anyone over, we seem to get no further than the main house."

"You mean you can't entertain privately?" Jennie asked in amazement. "When are you getting your own place? I mean, this is nice, but I remember you always dreaming how you'd decorate your own home."

"I know, we talked about it, but, well, as Wyatt said, these wings weren't being used and it seemed so logical when he explained—"

She rose and walked around restlessly, pausing only to light a cigarette. She was smoking too much, more than before, Jennie noticed.

"You mean you let that man talk you out of owning your own house?" Jennie said indignantly. "It isn't a case of money, is it? Surely, with a ranch this size, that shouldn't be a problem."

"It's nothing like that." She gazed out the window before turning to her cousin.

"You have to understand the setup, Jennie. They kid Wyatt about acting the overlord, but they'd do anything for him. Their parents died when Wyatt just graduated from college. He was twenty-one and suddenly head of a family and in charge of a struggling sheep ranch.

He kept the family together against all odds and has increased the ranch three-fold. It's one of the largest in the area. Fred is two years younger than he is, and Dave two more. He saw his brothers through college in spite of some pretty rough times.

"They idolize him, and I can't really blame them. The only trouble is he is so used to making all the decisions and keeping a tight rein on things, he forgets his brothers might have grown up and want something else." She stubbed out her cigarette, frowning over the mound in the ashtray. "It's all right with Dave. He loves this life, and Ruth is happy with it."

"And Fred?" Jennie asked softly.

Caroline tossed her head back with a hint of defiance. "He was content to go along with his brothers though he would have preferred a different life."

"If Fred doesn't like ranching, what does he want to do?" Jennie couldn't imagine him anywhere but here.

"Jewelry," was her surprising answer. "He creates the most fabulous designs. They tolerate his hobby but I at once saw how special they were. Even he doesn't realize how terrific they are."

"Is that necklace an example?" Jennie asked, leaning to examine the silver pendant.

Its design had caught her attention immediately.

She nodded, then went to her bedroom to return with a narrow suitcase. She placed it on the low table before Jennie and lifted the lid. White jewelry boxes were neatly aligned in the case.

One by one she held each one for inspection. Fred worked exclusively in silver. Each design was unique, many accented with unusual stones.

"He finds most of them on the ranch," Caroline explained. "Even these semiprecious ones. He's trying to show me how to recognize them in the rough. His brothers bring odd looking rocks. Fred grinds and polishes them, and they turn into these things of beauty. Aren't they fabulous?"

Jennie gazed admiringly at the collection of rings, bracelets and earrings. Anyone would be proud to own one of the dramatic necklaces.

"If I had a choice, I wouldn't know which one to choose," she admitted. It was hard to equate outdoorsman Fred with these sensitive creations.

Caroline fitted the covers back on the boxes. "That is the reason I was in Boise and not here when you arrived," she confessed. "I decided to take things into my own hands and packed what he had finished to take with me. I took them to the best jeweler in town. I struck it right. He was immediately impressed and said a buyer was in town checking on the local crafts. He made an appointment for me. Guess what! He wanted to buy everything at a pretty good price. He admitted the big cities are looking for things of this caliber. I haven't been a buyer for nothing. I realized if he was willing to pay so well, I could make direct contact with the stores and cut out the middleman."

Her face was lit with animation. This was the action she was used to and craved. No, the confining life of a rancher's wife was not for her, Jennie knew. It would corrode her love until there was nothing to keep them together. She loved her cousin too much to let that happen.

"Fred must have been thrilled with your news!" she enthused.

Caroline's face clouded, and she sank disconsolately into a chair.

"He was happy all right, but when I suggested it would mean leaving here so he could have the time to fill orders, he rebelled. Wyatt needed him, he said. Wyatt had sacrificed ten years of his life for them and he wasn't about to leave him. Can you beat that in this day and age? I told him there weren't indentured servants anymore, and he walked out of the room."

Caroline's hands went through her short cropped hair as she gave a helpless sigh.

"What do I do, Jennie? I'm crazy about the big dope but I'll smother if I remain here. You could learn to love this isolation, all writers are loners, but you know how I thrived on the excitement of my career. It isn't as if I was trying to coerce Fréd into something he didn't like. You should see him as he creates one of his masterpieces. He's a different person, all content within himself. I know that's what he'd love to do full time if only he didn't feel so darn obligated to his brother."

"I think it's cruel of Wyatt to expect his sacrifice," Jennie said, exasperated for her cousin. "It's downright feudal, but what I'd expect of him. Why don't you explain to his Lordship what you both want?"

Caroline's face twisted into a grimace. "I suggested that and it precipitated our first fight. I don't want to go through that again. I wouldn't dare do it on my own. Any announcement of that sort will have to come from Fred."

Jennie ached for her cousin. One person shouldn't have such control over the destiny of another. Drat the man. Caroline's problem added fuel to the resentment she already harbored.

"I shouldn't unload my problems on you, Jennie," she said somberly. "But I reached the point I had to talk to someone or explode. I tried to with Ruth. She's a dear, but we speak on different levels. She's such a complacent *hausfrau*, content with keeping her husband and children happy. She wouldn't understand what I need to exist. I want Fred happy also and I know he can't be, divided as he is. But how can I fight for him, for us, against someone so formidable as Wyatt?"

"What will you do next?" Jennie asked, skirting the question. She remembered all too well those blazing yellow eyes.

"I told Fred I was going to Dallas next week. I made an appointment with the buyer for Neiman-Marcus. If we get set in that prestigious store, you can bet doors will open in all the better places."

"How will you explain the trip to the family?"

"I have you. That's another reason I needed you to come now. I'll tell them I have to show you that section of Texas. You could be wanting more information for a novel, couldn't you?"

Jennie had to laugh at the mischievous glance her cousin gave. Leave it to her to expect her to concur with her devious ploys. Not that she minded. She had no reason to be loyal to the Dubrow family. In fact there were several reasons why she would gladly enter any scheme to break down the intimidating complacency of *that man*.

Ruth arrived late, missing the predinner cocktail, her face creased in a worried frown.

48

"Rudy is starting a cold, I'm afraid," she announced. "He has a slight temperature and is restless."

Wyatt was immediately alert. "Have you separated them?"

"It's a little late for that, I'm afraid," she said ruefully. "Rachel is sniffing already."

"You must stay away from them," he ordered. "We can't risk having you down with a cold. Why didn't you say something, Dave?"

His brother spread his hands in a gesture of innocence. "I was out with you, remember? I just showered and am hearing the news for the first time."

Jennie listened in surprise. Here was an excellent example how he took over and ordered the family about.

Reluctantly she had to admit Dave was acting complacently unalarmed. When Wyatt had warned he knew everything that happened around the ranch, the understanding was implicit he would take care of the problems also.

"Grace, the twins are coming down with a cold," he said as they sat down to dinner. "I want you to take complete care of them. We can't have Ruth sick. She's only up with the doctor's reluctant permission."

"Jennie and I will take over the kitchen as a stopgap, Wyatt," Caroline offered. "I know you have reason not to have faith in my cooking, but wait until you taste some of Jennie's concoctions."

His expression was carefully noncommittal. "I can hardly wait. I have survived this far so I suppose I'll be immune to anything else."

Caroline's wink stopped the sharp retort rising in Jennie.

"Yes, you men have proved you have cast-iron systems. Anything we produce won't make a dent," she said slyly, widening apparently innocent eyes while looking at him."

Fred hid his smile, remembering gourmet meals he had enjoyed in the apartment prepared by Jennie.

"The twins always bounce back quickly from these things," Ruth said hopefully. "I feel terrible being so useless."

"Hey, none of that," Dave said gently, his big calloused hand reaching for his wife's. "Your job is the most important one of all."

Jennie swallowed hard, seeing the love given and received. Yes, to them creating a new life was vastly important. Procreation was a vital part of life here, whether human or the sheep.

Was it important to Fred? Caroline, she knew, seldom responded to children. If they had one, it would be enough, and she guessed from Fred's reaction to the twins, he would be satisfied with that limit.

Wyatt, however, would demand the right to

father a small brood. Anyone so vitally alive would desire a houseful of husky sons with a sprinkling of daughters. She had seen his joy when playing with the twins.

"Thank you for your offer to help," Wyatt said later as Jennie went upstairs. "I don't usually ask guests to do kitchen duty. A simple breakfast will do. Plenty of hot coffee and toast will fill the corners."

"I'll make a try at some eggs. If the yolks break, I can always scramble them," said Jennie sweetly, turning away so Wyatt missed her sly smile.

Chapter Four

By the time Caroline came into the kitchen, Jennie had the iron pans heating in the oven for the popovers and the coffee starting to perk. She had found a ricer, and was making her version of Eggs Mimossa, an eye appealing dish.

"You can set the table," Jennie said, stirring the sauce.

"Thanks for the easy job," Caroline replied sleepily. "Let's splurge and use the good china. I'm tired of the heavy ironstone china we use in the kitchen. Besides, if you're making what I think, the best is none too good. I wouldn't miss this for the world," she grinned. "I made Fred promise to say nothing about your cooking. We can't wait until Wyatt tastes this meal!"

Fred came in, sniffing in anticipation. "What heaven! Notice how early I am. I aim to savor every nuance as Wyatt starts in."

He gave Jennie a hug, and Caroline laughed as she poured his coffee.

Jennie's laugh froze in her throat as she met yellow hawkeyes. Wyatt stood in the door and any warmth she had felt from Fred's greeting quickly dispersed under his cold condemnation.

Mr. Know-it-all, she fumed helplessly as she turned to the stove. If she let her anger rise, it would reflect in her cooking, and now, more than ever, she meant to have that arrogant man eat humble pie. She had been on the receiving end of his malice too long.

The popovers couldn't have been higher or flakier, the sauce for the chopped egg whites was just the right consistency, and she added the mushrooms and cubed cheese before ricing the egg yolk over the top. Thick slices of ham were still moist with edges just beginning to curl.

For an anxious moment, she was afraid she hadn't made enough. Fred buttered the last popover, admitting he had no room for it but pronounced it would be criminal to leave it behind.

Ruth and David were highly vocal in their praise, but Wyatt said nothing until he finished the last of his coffee.

He looked across the table, taking in her face still flushed from the oven heat and extravagant words.

"I've been listening to the glowing words of appreciation," he said slowly. "There's nothing I can add. The question comes to mind, however, how can you top this?"

The laugh was general as they rose and left to do their chores. The house seemed strangely empty without them.

Ruth sat at the kitchen table lining slices of bread to make sandwiches.

"The men won't be able to come for lunch," she explained. "They are checking on an irrigation pump. Wyatt intends to fly over some new land he bought to see if it needs spraying to get rid of the sagebrush."

"You have an airplane?" Jennie asked in surprise.

"Yes, Wyatt bought one several years ago. It's the only way to check this large a place. I don't know exactly how many thousand acres we have now. Old Tom Brenner died last year and Wyatt bought the spread from the heirs. They weren't interested in it. He let it run down when he got old and the sagebrush has taken hold again.

"We're lucky to get it because it has a dependable mountain stream which runs for a piece before the desert claims it. They've put in a dam and a pump for irrigation and hope the result will be worth the expense. We need more winter pasture."

Her face was lit with pride for the men who had successfully won another battle against a rugged environment.

Caroline took her down in the root cellar.

Sacks of potatoes and onions were in the cool room. Airtight bins held flour and sugar, and stacked cartons of canned vegetables and fruit lined one wall.

"You saw the so-called town," she said disparagingly.

Jennie had. The two-pump station was backed by a small general store which also held the post office. Besides a few small houses, that was it. A stop on the two-lane road was ignored on most maps.

"A truck goes once a month into one of the larger towns for supplies and comes back loaded," she explained.

"Several of the ranchers have their own planes," she continued. "A friend was flying into Boise and I grabbed the opportunity to hitch a ride. That's why I had to leave, even though I was afraid you might arrive early."

Jennie was beginning to have an understanding of the tremendous problems of running a ranch in this remote area. Wyatt might farm out some responsibilities, but he would never release control. He should have a wife who could relieve him of the immediate problems at the homestead. The thought became a question.

"Wyatt is in his early thirties, isn't he? Has he ever been married?"

"No, though I understand he was on the verge when the folks died. He gave up any idea of marriage when faced with bringing the ranch back on its feet and getting his brothers through college. They wanted to quit and help him, but he insisted they have the same education he had."

Jennie grudgingly gave him credit for his sacrifice. But she wondered what type of woman had given him up, letting him struggle by himself. She would have insisted upon working by the side of the man she loved.

"I hate to ask you to do this," Ruth said before going for her prescribed midmorning rest. "Pedro was supposed to stop by to take the lunches to the men, but he's off in town to pick up the part for your car. Can you take these to them? They should be at the barn."

Jennie readily agreed. She hadn't seen anything of the ranch except views from the windows—and that fateful excursion out into the moonlight.

The sun beat down on her as she hurried to the barn. The intensity surprised her this late in fall. She couldn't get used to the heat during the day especially after the heavy chill at night.

Now under its glare, she could only think of the relief offered by the barn. If it was this bad now, how had city-loving Caroline endured the summer!

She passed the corral. Several horses were cropping the grass and she thought she recognized Devil. He was a powerful beast. He raised his head to give her an arrogant stare.

Dave was loading a half-truck with an assortment of pipes while Fred checked through a tool locker attached to one side.

"Don't ever leave the house without a hat," Dave admonished, seeing her pause to adjust her vision to the sudden gloom in the barn. "In fact, you should wear dark glasses also until you get used to our sun."

"Now you tell me," she grimaced, handing them the lunches. "Ruth sent me with these."

"Thanks for bringing them" Fred said, "We're running late, and it saves a trip back to the house. Want to run Wyatt's to him?" He pointed out the doors to where he was checking the motor of a small two-seater Cessna.

She would have liked to refuse, but she obliged.

Wyatt's gaze was piercing, taking in her heat flushed cheeks.

"I know," she forestalled him. "I was just informed I shouldn't challenge the sun without hat and glasses. Ruth sent your lunch. When will you be back?"

"I should be back by early afternoon," he replied. "That's the blessing of a plane. By horse it would be an overnight trip, and the truck would bounce our brains loose, not to mention what it would do to the suspension system. Have you ever flown in one of these?"

"No," she admitted. "Though small planes have fascinated me."

"Tell Cary you're coming with me," he said

abruptly. "Borrow a hat and glasses. You'll need a scarf also."

She hesitated, the last olive branch had proved to have thorns. Could she trust him this time? Still, if she refused, he would never give her a second invitation, and her natural curiosity won.

"I'll be right back," she said, giving a wide grin in anticipation of the adventure.

His eyes were shuttered as he watched her swinging stride, the dark hair glistening in the sunlight as the breeze lifted it from her shoulders. She looked very much like her cousin, but there the resemblance faltered. He had worried when first introduced to his new sister-in-law. She was a true city girl, and he doubted she could settle for the country life. It would have been better if Fred had chosen this one. Wyatt frowned as he finished checking the motor.

The take-off was bumpy across the rough ground, but before Jennie could be frightened, the plane lifted and they circled slowly around the house before angling toward the low butte which protected them from the prevailing winter winds.

The motor's noise dampened conversation, but Wyatt pointed out features displayed below. A large herd of sheep was being collected.

"For market," he mouthed.

She nodded her understanding. There hadn't seemed to be many animals around, scattered as they were, but below they were massed into lumpy relief. A foreshortened man waved, and two black dots proved to be dogs dashing after reluctant sheep.

A narrow stream flowed through the center of the small valley, and Wyatt pointed to where they had dammed the exit to create a pond. It was from there the precious water came to irrigate the nearby pastureland where the sheep were rotated for final fattening before shipment to market.

The plane climbed over the top of the butte, barren except for the ever encroaching sagebrush.

Jennie was struck by the contrast of the land now spread beneath her. To her untrained eye, the browns and tans meant desert land broken only by occasional clumps of cottonwood trees clinging to by now dry stream beds. How did those scattered clumps of sheep survive?

Questions rose, but she'd have to wait until they landed for the answers.

Ahead a dark shadow lay across the land. As they approached, she saw it was the blackened scar of a range fire. She glanced at him in consternation. Had he lost many sheep? There was no way to stop a fire out here if it once became out of control.

Wyatt dropped close to the ground, and Jennie saw he was following a trail directly below. When a stretch was relatively straight, he dipped the plane, and they were bumping over the uneven terrain. She hadn't had time to be frightened when he leaned over and unsnapped her seat belt.

"Time to stretch our legs," he said, helping her down. "I want to check the results of the burn."

"You mean you set this fire on purpose?" she asked. "And here I was worried you might have lost some sheep in a range fire!"

"Old Tom let the place run down the last years of his life," Wyatt explained. "It doesn't take long for the sagebrush to take hold. We control-burned it this spring, and I'm checking to see if it's done a good enough job so we can save the expense of a spraying. This was Tom's best pastureland, and I'd like to use it next year."

Jennie looked in surprise at the sparse growth. This was his best pastureland? What a waste of money!

His eyes crinkled, reading her thoughts. "Don't turn your nose up at it, Jennie girl," he smiled grimly. "If all my ranch land was this good, I'd have no worries."

"But how can sheep exist," she exploded. "Surely they need water to survive, and this—"

She looked despairingly at the autumn brown stubble of grass poking through the blackened remains of the sagebrush.

"Sheep don't need as much water as cattle. That's why this is sheep country. There are enough water holes to take care of their needs."

Jennie was struggling to understand his reasoning for staying on this harsh land. Surely there were greener valleys!

"What is the challenge?" she asked at last. "I mean, I've driven through lush green country where you wouldn't have to worry about water and the battle of sagebrush. Why live here where it is so desolate?"

She was thinking of Caroline's welfare. There were larger towns in those valleys. She wouldn't feel so cut off from the life she craved.

Wyatt didn't answer and she looked at him, wondering if he had heard.

He was staring over the miles of undulating land. His features never looked more hawk-like with yellow eyes piercing the distance. Finally he turned to her. "Is that how it looks to you, desolate and featureless" he asked. "Don't you see the richness of the colors, the silvery grays and purples, the subtle browns and tans? Have you ever seen a blue sky like this over Chicago?"

He gave a shrug and moved a step away. To

Jennie, that step was a mile. She had failed him, and she gazed around again, trying to see the land through his eyes.

A breeze found them, standing in the shade of the plane. It was cooler on this higher plateau, and she breathed deeply of its purity. No acid gas fumes from lanes of traffic. No greasy cooking smells exuding from exhaust fans. The silence was as intimidating as the vastness of the land spread at her feet. The mountains, hinting of the Cascade Range beyond, were blue-tinged in the shadows.

This was Wyatt country. He was part of it, and she knew he could never leave it and be whole.

He had moved on, bending to tug at a clump of grass, kicking at the thin layer of soil. He left her, checking what his next move would be to reclaim the land.

She leaned against the plane, letting her senses take over. Slowly the undulating land spoke, its rich earth tones becoming a tapestry beguiling to the eye. To her ears came the harmony of the faint rustling of grasses, the muted rubbings of the crickets, the faraway warning cry of some small ground animal.

It was all alien to her city bred senses, but during the half hour Wyatt moved over the area, it had cast its spell, a spell which still held her when Wyatt checked her safety straps when they settled in their seats.

"I understand now," she murmured, as if to herself.

His glance was sharp as he took in her bemused expression. Her soft lips were parted as if still drinking in the wonder.

His hand went to her face, and he ran a finger along her cheek. Startled, she met his gaze, and for one heart-stopping moment, time was suspended. Then his lips were on hers.

"Don't look too long, Jennie," he said softly. "Or you won't be able to leave." His hand dropped and he started the engine.

He flew in a wide zigzag course while sweeping the area below with a piercing stare. What was he looking for?

Now Jennie gazed below with a new insight. She admired the pale brushes of yellow where the sagebrush offered a last bloom. Magenta streaks indicated the spread of Russian thistle. The ivory of the grass seed heads was almost luminous under the sun's reflection. How could she have thought the landscape colorless! It was varied as a painting, dabbed in subtle tints and shades.

He pointed to a clump of trees, and the plane dipped as he searched for the best approach. Again the plane bumped upon landing, but she was prepared for it now, confident in the pilot.

His hands were on her waist, helping her

out, and she slid down to rest against his muscle hard body.

Her heart thudded erratically at the unexpected electric shock. They both stepped apart, eyeing each other warily. Then she was backed against the plane, his hands on her shoulders, gliding up to lift her face as they cupped under her chin. It was not the brutal kiss of the first night; he did not have to bind her with arms of steel. She had no desire to struggle.

A hint of a smile softened his mouth as he stared down at her, his yellow hawkeyes bright but unrevealing.

She fought a need to run, even while reasoning she was overreacting to a kiss. The Dubrow men emanated too much animal magnetism. To be ensnared by this man would be like being caught in a whirlpool. Even to ride the outer rim could be fatal.

She had no desire to test her luck. He could fascinate, but her first instinct to distrust was still strong, and she confounded herself by walking calmly away, as if cataclysmic kisses were common to her.

"Time for lunch, Jennie," Wyatt called a few minutes later.

He had spread an old blanket under a tree where a glint of water ran through a grassy bed.

"I never expected water here," she said in surprise.

"A subterranean stream emerges here," he said, pointing to an outcropping of rocks where the water bubbled noisily. "It only lasts a hundred feet and submerges again. It's not deep, but much more important, it's constant. It's the main watering hole for the area and makes this section valuable for grazing."

"I was wondering how the trees survived. What a blessing they must be to your shepherds!"

She sat on the blanket and he offered her a sandwich.

"I never thought to bring my own," Jennie apologized.

"Ruth always packs more than we need," he assured her.

She admitted she had thought four sandwiches, a thick wedge of cake and two apples had seemed like a lot, but she had seen how they ate. He gallantly offered her the first drink of coffee from the top of the thermos.

"How much land do you have?" she asked, watching several small dust devils swirl in the distance. The plane had traveled in sweeping curves, and she had no idea how much ground they had covered.

"A little over twenty thousand acres, but I can't pinpoint the exact amount," he admitted with a laugh. "These old deeds never were surveyed accurately. They'd run from water hole to rock outcroppings or stream beds. Then during a severe winter, the snow would carry off the rocks or cause a slide. A water hole would dry up and hopefully reappear nearby. And a spring runoff might change a creek's course. So it's give or take a few hundred acres."

"Doesn't that cause friction with the neighbors?" she asked. In westerns, many range wars were caused by boundary disputes.

He gave a slight shrug. "A lot isn't worth fighting over, but, yes, the question has come up. We ranchers have decided to fly in surveyors."

His eyes roved over this land he loved. His face was in repose, softening the hawk-like features. The lips now were not the usual tight controlled line but revealed an unexpected sensuous fullness that quickened Jennie's pulse.

Perhaps they could be tender and sharing after all, joining in a kiss of love instead of that insistent male demand.

She shivered in remembrance even while conscious of an anticipation for more. This man was entering her thoughts too much!

"Will you be all right alone?" he asked. "I want to scout around for about half an hour. There's been an increase in rustling. That's one reason I took the plane. I can check a larger area to see if there has been any activity on the ranch. Don't wander away. You don't know the land, and I'd hate to have you turn an ankle on these stones or get hurt if you fell into a ravine."

"I won't move," she promised, gathering the remains from the lunch and putting them in the carry bag.

She watched him until he disappeared as the land dipped. What a different man he was here! This land was a study in contrasts, but no more than that ambivalent man.

A silence moved in, a silence never more complete. The heat had made her drowsy. She stretched out on the blanket to lazily watch the leaves answer the caress of the breeze. Soon she was asleep.

She felt the soft brush of lips. He was lying half over her, his heart beat strong on her breast. She met the question in his hawk-eyes, and her hand went of its own volition to the nape of his neck.

The kiss was as tender as she had anticipated, and her hand crept into the thick wiry hair, as alive as the man.

His fingertips roved gently along the curve of her neck, and the tenderness was drowned as passion won. The buttons of her shirt were opened and his hand moved caressingly over her breasts, arousing them to full response with each stroke.

His mouth followed the trail of his hands until she moaned as the ache in her grew in a sweeping surge. She was helpless in her need even as she fought the desire.

She gave one final effort at control. "No!" she cried. . . .

Blinking against the sun shooting a hole in the canopy, she gazed up at the man standing at the edge of the blanket. His eyes were the unrevealing stare of a hawk, and she blinked again. The thunder of her heartbeat receded as the dream faded. Cheeks flushed, she rolled over to sit up.

How long had he been standing there? Had she cried aloud in her sleep? For one instant she thought she had caught an answering flame deep in those yellow eyes.

"I didn't mean to fall asleep," she murmured, sweeping her hair back with one hand. "How long were you gone?"

"About half an hour." He hunched down beside her, placing a walnut sized red stone in her hand.

"I bring untold riches," he grinned, meeting her questioning glance. "It's a garnet. I haven't found one this size in a long time."

She held the rough stone up to the sun, admiring the deep glowing color. "I heard Oregon was a rock hound's paradise," she commented, balancing the stone on her ring finger. "It would make an eye-popping ring. How large would it be when polished?"

"Depends on the impurities," he said, re-

trieving the stone and placing it in his pocket.
"Don't tell me you'd be satisfied with anything
less than a diamond!"

She met his mocking gaze. "If the man I
loved found a stone like that, it would mean
much more than any store diamond," she said
defiantly.

A smile lifted the corners of his mouth.
"When you find him, I'll be only too happy to
take him on a gem hunt. But now we better
head home." He offered his hand to help her
up.

She hid a shiver. In her dream that hand
had moved knowingly.

The trip back was swift. She thanked him
for the outing and hurried to the house. Dinner depended upon her.

The quartered chickens were seasoned and
floured before being placed in the oven. Later,
special herbs would be added to the cream to
make her tasty version of gravy. A rice pilaf
and slivered carrots touched with nutmeg
would complete the menu.

This is what she enjoyed doing, and she
hummed contentedly as she sliced tomatoes
into a bowl to marinade.

"I'm supposed to be working on the books
but these smells are driving me wild!" Wyatt
said from the doorway.

She lifted several slices on a plate and
handed them to him. "They're better after

soaking a while," she said. "But this cook enjoyed her afternoon too much to worry about an extra hour to marinade."

The words were barely out when she recalled the heart-stopping moment when pulsing lips had clung hungrily together. The oven door was open and she hoped the resulting flush to her cheeks would be attributed to the heat.

Caroline came in from setting the table in the dining room. "I figured it's about time that room had some use," she said, eyeing Wyatt with a hint of defiance.

"By all means," he said, dipping into the bowl for more tomato slices. "We always had our meals there before the folks died. It only became too much of an effort for the slapdash meals I made later." He shrugged wide shoulders. "Bachelors learn to do without such niceties. However, Jennie has given me an idea. Jennie, we could use a full-time cook. I'll change the spare bedroom into a study and you can concentrate there on your writing. My one request is that you take over the kitchen at dinnertime. We can struggle through the other meals. How does that sound to you all?"

"That doesn't sound fair to Jennie," Caroline protested, filling the mugs with coffee as they settled around the kitchen table. "She has other attributes and shouldn't be buried out here. There's no one here for her to meet.

You don't want her to end up a dried up old maid, do you?"

Wyatt raised a mocking eyebrow. "I can't envision such a fate for our Jennie." He pushed back his chair. "Back to the books," he said. "The damn paper work gets more involved every year."

"Do you think Grace minds my taking over the kitchen?" Jennie asked after Wyatt had left the room.

Caroline lifted her shoulders in a shrug. "Wyatt orders. We obey."

Her antagonism showed and Jennie looked at her cousin with compassion. She was indeed faced with a formidable opponent if she intended to tackle her brother-in-law!

"Don't worry about Grace," Caroline continued. "She's never really liked cooking anyway and would much prefer to concentrate on the twins. Besides, now that everyone has tasted your cooking, I doubt they will be satisfied with anything else. Wyatt made that quite plain. You'll find that he may well turn the spare bedroom into a workroom for you. My experience has been that he always means what he says."

Jennie raised startled eyes. "You don't really believe that arrogant man could induce me to stay!" she cried. "True, he was very civil today, but I'm only counting that as a truce while I do kitchen duty. You have no idea how he spoke to me when I first came. I fully expect the same treatment when he discovers why I've gone to Texas with you. In fact, if I didn't need to pick up my car, I wouldn't ever come back here at all."

Ruth hurried in, pausing at the stove to pour coffee.

"I'll take this to Grace before coming for mine," she said, a worried frown creasing her brow. "I don't like the way the twins are. It looks like more than a cold. Is Wyatt around? I better check if he thinks we should call a doctor."

"Can't you call without his approval?" Jennie asked. Here again was evidence of the tight control he held over everyone.

Ruth looked at her in surprise. "Yes, I guess so," she said, "I just don't want to act the overanxious mother."

"Bill Brown is a doctor who retired nearby," Caroline explained. "He helps out in emergencies. The ranchers respect his retirement, so call him only if necessary."

Jennie berated herself. There she jumped to conclusions again, trying to find black marks to hold against the man. What was there about him that put her on the defensive?

They heard Wyatt accompany Ruth to the west wing. When they returned, he went to the phone. Caroline placed a mug of coffee in Ruth's hands.

"He thinks it might be the flu," Ruth said worriedly.

The men came in and she flew to her husband, crying out the news. His arm went around her as they listened to what was decided over the phone.

How wonderful to have someone with whom to share life's worries and joys, Jennie thought, and for the first time wondered over her single state.

"Bill agrees it sounds like the flu," Wyatt returned to report to them all. "He prescribed the usual aspirin and rest. And don't worry, Ruth," he added reassuringly, "if they don't show improvement by noon tomorrow, I'll fly them to the hospital."

Ruth smiled shakily. "I feel so helpless having to stay away from them when they need me most. Thank goodness for Grace."

"Let's hope she doesn't come down with the bug," Dave said.

Jennie fixed a tray for Grace so she could stay with the fretful children and Caroline offered to take it to her.

"Can't have our chief cook catch the bug," she said. "I'm more expendable."

Wyatt's look was thoughtful as he watched Caroline go with the food. He must be wondering how she meant that, Jennie thought. He was constantly alert, ever the guardian over Dubrow Ranch and its occupants.

She was surprised by the comfort of the thought.

All conflict was forgotten as they sat down to dinner. Caroline had gone all out to dress up the table. Long forgotten silver candlesticks had been polished, and the old-fashioned ornate flatware gleamed with a sedate elegance.

"I forgot how handsome the old heirlooms were," Dave said with appreciation. "What gives? Are we announcing any earthshaking event? Another addition to the family, perhaps, or an engagement?" He grinned, eyeing his brothers teasingly.

"I felt it my duty to set a table equal to what Jennie has prepared," Caroline said lightly. "You've been sniffing at the kitchen door, now wait until you taste!"

The meal was an unqualified success. Not one grain of rice was left and two pies disappeared before Jennie's unbelieving eyes.

"Jennie," Fred begged. "Do you think you could teach Cary some of these recipes before you leave?"

"I warned you before we were married I had no love for the kitchen," she reminded him. "Besides, Jennie gave up on me long ago."

"But I could never decorate like you do," Jennie returned loyally. "Our apartment was just as striking as what you've done here."

Goaded by she knew not what, she looked to the man at the head of the table. "Don't you think Caroline has done an outstanding job in her wing? Why don't you have her redecorate these rooms?"

His eyes were instantly shuttered. "You see a need to change things?" he asked coolly.

Jennie lowered her lashes. Flushed by the success of her cooking, she had been indiscreet. He was right to reject her question.

But then she thought of her unhappy cousin. The challenge of redecorating these rooms would perhaps ease her restlessness. In spite of her brave words about getting Fred to move, she had not had much success in doing so.

"Every house needs an occasional face-lift," she said apologetically.

"And after being here two days, you've decided it was time for us to have one." The cool censure in his voice made her wince.

"The girl's right," Fred boomed fearlessly into the breach. "We've changed nothing since the folks died. We've become so used to it, we haven't noticed how shabby things are getting."

"I know Cary has excellent taste," Wyatt returned, his gaze never leaving Jennie's face. "What about you? Do you have any ideas?"

Jennie looked to her cousin for help, but for some unknown reason met only amusement there. Heavens, what had she gotten into!

She tossed her head in defiance as she met

75

his gaze. "I dare say most women redecorate a room when they first see it. It's part of their makeup."

A faint smile curved his lips. "That would be another way to keep you here a little longer," he murmured. "I'm certain the family is behind me in voting to keep you closeted in the kitchen."

"Here, here!" Dave seconded enthusiastically.

She glanced around the table, unable to comprehend the amusement evident on everyone's face.

"Cary, do you think you can do the dishes?" Wyatt said, rising. "Fred can help. Jennie deserves a rest."

Fred made a face but rose good naturedly; but Jennie rebelled.

"We women will clean up," she said firmly. "You men have worked hard enough all day."

Ruth and Dave had left, anxious to be near their children. That would mean she would be alone with Wyatt, and that had to be avoided at all costs. She had an uneasy feeling he would make her pay for her defiance about redecorating, and she wasn't about to give him the opportunity.

The cousins spent a cheerful hour exchanging gossip. Jennie filled in the latest about mutual friends in Chicago.

"I should have contacted more people before coming," she apologized. "You know how I'm isolated on my cloud while writing."

The last pot was put away when Fred came in to check progress.

"Wyatt's back at the desk tackling the paper work," he said cheerfully. "Thank goodness he's better at math than Dave or I and has taken over that headache."

"I should do some also," Caroline admitted. "Jennie and I are leaving in two days and I have to check if my presentation is letter perfect." She hung up the towels to dry and pointed to the bag of garbage. "That's your detail, love. You'll excuse me, Jennie? I must get this done."

Jennie waved her on, wiping the stove top. They left on their separate missions, and she finished her job, wondering sadly if her cousin was doing the best thing by pushing Fred further along the path she desired. Having lived and loved this open land, could he exist contentedly in the confines of a city? Caroline would inch him closer and closer until they lived in a large metropolis where she could be happy.

Thank goodness she hadn't married the older brother! A bulldozer wouldn't move him from his beloved ranch!

A packet of carrot peelings sat by a cabinet. She had forgotten to throw it in the trash, and now hurried into a jacket to get rid of it.

"Fred?" she called tentatively. She had no idea where the garbage was deposited.

A bundled figure moved from the shadow of a small clump of lodgepole pines. "Looking for me?" he asked.

"A small additional offering," she answered. "Where does one put it?"

"I'll show you," he said, taking her arm to steer her over the night shrouded ground. "We don't have the conveniences here of city collections. When the cans are full, we truck them to a dumping ground and burn it."

They stopped as he opened a gate to a small enclosure.

"We're only fooling ourselves with this fencing," he laughed, taking the bundle and depositing it in one of the trash cans. A rock was placed on the lid. "That's another idle gesture. When the coyotes and other assortment of night prowlers decide they want a snack, this stops them for only a minute."

They paused at the edge of the shadows, and Jennie again was overwhelmed by the moonlit display. Only this time she could enjoy it fully, she told herself. With Wyatt, she had been on guard against an overbearing man.

Again she was filled with awe over the silvery majesty of the scene. *Yes, Wyatt, I can understand why you love it!* It was a good thing she was moving on before it took hold of her.

Fred was staring over the silvered pasture toward the distant mountains. "What do you think of Cary's scheme?" he asked quietly.

"You mean selling your jewelry?" she returned. "I never suspected how gifted you were, Fred! Caroline has a sixth sense about fashion trends, as well as being a good businesswoman. You couldn't find a better agent to handle your work."

"It is only a hobby," he said. "She wants to make it more."

"Yes, she told me."

"It would mean leaving this." His hand moved to the view before them.

"And Wyatt," she added meaningly.

His sigh breathed a cloud of moisture into the cold night air. "Yes, and Wyatt."

She could feel sorry for the man's dilemma, but her loyalty to her cousin won. "Caroline would be happier in the city."

"I know." Again the sigh steamed the air. "I did some mighty fast talking to get her to marry me. She warned she loved city life, but would try living here for a year."

Jennie glanced at him in surprise. This was the first she heard of that promise.

"The year is only half over," she murmured.

He did not have to answer. They both knew another year, or ten, would make no difference. His wife would never be content here.

"City living has big pluses," she offered carefully.

"I wouldn't mind it," he said surprisingly. "What I've tasted while at college showed me the resources could inspire me in my work."

"Then why the reluctance to leave?" She had to ask, even though she knew the answer.

"I owe Wyatt my allegiance," he said somberly. It rang like a pledge, and Jennie could appreciate the depth of Caroline's problem.

"There comes a time when a man's allegiance belongs to himself and his wife," she said tartly. How had Wyatt inspired such devotion from his brothers? Poor Caroline! She was fighting a lonely battle. No wonder she had begged Jennie to visit her! And she had been right. If it meant toppling Lord Wyatt, she had picked the right person. Jennie would be glad to help her!

A mournful sob sounded in the distance. Abject loneliness hung in the wail. Jennie gasped.

The answering cry was much closer. The forlorn howl made Jennie shiver. Could anything be that heartrendingly hopeless?

"Hey, city girl, it's only the coyotes!" Fred mocked, feeling her tremble. With a quiet chuckle, he drew her protectively close.

The vague, haunting unrest the drawn-out cry had evoked, disappeared. Arm in arm, Jennie and Fred walked slowly toward the house.

The windows of the library which Wyatt used as his office were dimly lit by the lamp on his desk. She faltered for a moment, seeing the ominously outlined figure, black against the light.

Had he observed them, also highlighted by the moonlight? Had he seen them walking close together? What would his reaction be? He had warned her once, and would show no mercy. She couldn't bear to think of their next encounter.

The rest of the evening was long and uncomfortable. She was shiveringly aware of the man working in the next room, afraid he would join them around the fireplace.

When she finally closed the door to her bedroom, it was with relief. So far she had escaped a confrontation.

But what of tomorrow?

Chapter Five

At breakfast Dave's face was lined with concern. "I'm afraid Ruth has the bug," he announced. "She has a slight temperature and admits to feeling achy."

Wyatt was immediately by his side, and they went to check the extent of the illness.

"What if we all get the flu!" Caroline groaned.

Jennie understood the reason for her distraction. If they became sick, how soon could she set up another appointment?

She was certain under Caroline's persuasion, her husband would make the change she desired, especially after his confession last night admitting he was not adverse to the life-style she craved.

No way was she going to be around when the bomb exploded when they told Big Brother they would leave. Her car had to be finished when they returned.

She remembered she had cuddled the children shortly before the first symptoms appeared. "I'm the one who might be next," she confessed, and told Caroline her suspicions.

"You can't," Caroline said firmly, as if the words had the power to stop any possible spread of the infection. "If I don't make these appointments, it will be twice as hard to get another. You have no idea what prima donnas these buyers can be."

"Don't you realize if Ruth comes down with the bug, one of us will have to stay to do the cooking?" Jennie replied just as firmly. "Grace will have to nurse her as well as the children. We can't go off and leave the men adrift. Wyatt will cut you in little pieces." Not to mention what he would do to her.

"But you shouldn't take on this burden. You're a guest," she protested.

Jennie's smile mocked her. "You mean you will handle the cooking?"

Caroline raised her hands in a gesture of helplessness. "That would be a catastrophe. You win. I'll stop being selfish."

"There is no reason you have to stay," Jennie protested. "I can handle the cooking."

Caroline hugged her cousin. "You're a love, Jennie. I always seem to be taking advantage of you, but one of these days I'll stop thinking about myself and concentrate on finding you a man as wonderful as mine."

Jennie returned the hug, hoping the spasm

of pain running across her face was unnoticed.

The men returned and Jennie hurriedly served the breakfast. While they ate, she filled the trays for the children and Grace, adding another for Ruth.

"She's got to stay in bed?" she asked Dave.

"Yes," he answered glumly. "Wyatt called Doc Brown, and he promised to come later."

"Well, at least our gourmet cook is still hale and hearty," Fred said, smiling warmly at Jennie.

"Caroline's cousin is here on a brief visit and plans to leave shortly," Wyatt said stiffly, reaching for another slice of French toast.

He can't even call me by my name, Jennie raged silently. *He's making me a non-person.*

"We've already discussed it," Caroline said quickly. "Jennie has volunteered to handle the cooking chores until everyone is back to normal."

"That's a relief," Dave said. "Ruth's appetite has been poor enough without being sick. I was counting on Jennie's expertise to stimulate it."

The yellow eyes finally looked at her, coldly condemning, unblinkingly hawk-like as they pierced her. "She seems to have a great deal of expertise in many things," he enunciated slowly.

No one seemed to notice the disdain in his

voice as the words dropped on her like weighted stones.

So he *had* seen them last night. She was condemned without being given a recourse to prove her innocence! She fumed over the injustice of his interpretation. Just because he took what he wanted didn't mean his gentle brother reacted the same way.

Her hand shook so it was a minute before she could turn the last of the French toast in the skillet. What had she done, tying herself here for an unlimited time! For her cousin's sake she would have to tolerate the whiplash of his temper. But before she left, she vowed, he'd pay for her discomfort!

"For heaven's sake, you're not feeding an army!" Caroline cried later in the afternoon. "Drop everything and come outside for some fresh air. We love your cooking, doll, but we don't want to be responsible for your collapse!"

Jennie agreed, feeling suddenly tired. She'd have to get more sleep if she continued like this.

"Better put on a jacket," Caroline advised. "Our hot days are over, thank goodness, but I don't know if I like the cold front coming through any better." She picked a jacket off a hanger and handed it to Jennie, saving her the trip upstairs. It was one of the men's and she laughed as she snuggled into the voluminous folds.

"I'm all packed. Now I only have to convince Fred I should go."

Jennie gave a crooked smile. "You have any doubts about your ability?"

A little laugh bubbled up. "Not really. He's a big teddy bear. I have no problems until I attempt to interfere with his misplaced sense of loyalty to his brother."

"Still, you have to admire him for it."

"Yes. It's aggravating, though I respect it," Caroline admitted. "When you hear some of the hardships Wyatt went through in the beginning, you wonder what drove him to hang on to his inheritance. Their father was a dreamer and the ranch was pretty debt ridden. I understand one of the ranchers, a Basil Franjule, helped him out when the bank wanted to foreclose. It was around then Lorraine became number one."

"Lorraine?"

They had walked to the little stream running from the small dammed pool. A leaf floated onto the water and spun dizzily on its way.

"Lorraine Franjule. They're a Basque family who own the next ranch. I've heard talk papa wanted this place while daughter wanted the owner, and it looked like both would get what they wanted. Wyatt managed to pay off the debt and somehow lost the daughter in the process."

Jennie pretended interest in a colored rock. "Is she the one he was engaged to?"

Caroline frowned while searching her memory. "I don't remember hearing it actually got that far. One minute they were a hot number, then the next she was off, married a friend of a cousin who was visiting. I heard the catty remark he was a good catch, and Lorraine wasn't one to miss a golden opportunity."

"Was she pretty?" Why was she asking these questions? They had nothing to do with her. It must be her writer's instinct searching for story threads to weave into some future novel.

"Yes, stunning, in a Spanish way," Caroline confessed. "I never met her, of course, but Fred showed me some of the family albums one night and she was in a few pictures."

Was this why the mighty Wyatt acted so antagonistic to her? Had he been so angry to be spurned by a woman in those lean, hard years that now he trusted no woman?

She gave a silent, bitter laugh over her romantic woolgathering. Whoever Lorraine was, she was a lucky girl to have escaped him!

She looked back to the house. It blended serenely into the landscape. Who would expect the turmoil its owner could raise in her with the arching of one disdainful eyebrow? Never had she disliked a man so much, and never had she felt so trapped by circumstances. Why in heaven's name hadn't she remained safe in Chicago?

"Is it possible to climb the hill behind the house?" she asked. She needed a change of subject to wipe Wyatt from her mind.

"That's a butte," Caroline corrected. "Flat top, steep sides. Yes, there is a way. The trail starts on the north side. Fred threatens to take me up but so far I've been able to beg off because of the heat."

"It's not very high. It looks like an easy challenge."

The fine boned nose, so like her own, wrinkled. "It's a challenge I'm not interested in taking, though Fred says the view from the top is outstanding. Don't you try it on your own, Miss Daredevil. I'll tell Wyatt to take you if you must try."

"No, thank you," Jennie replied dryly. "Your brother-in-law resents me enough without taking him from his work."

"You've noticed it then," Caroline said, eyeing her with speculation. "He's never been so caustic to anyone. I asked Fred what gives but he's bewildered by the reaction. Surely, he should be over that to-do about Devil."

Jennie gave an elaborate shrug. She knew why, all right. He was busy thinking he had to protect his brothers from her fatal charms.

"He was polite enough when invited on his

plane, but I seem to rub him the wrong way when here. The obvious solution is to stay away which is what I intend to do."

She had to—it was a case of survival. She didn't care to be flayed any further.

A car traveled up the driveway, trailing a long dust streamer.

"It's Doc Brown," Caroline announced, squinting into the sunlight. "Let's get back. I don't know if the men will see his trail."

He was everyone's picture of a family doctor. Medium height, bushy gray hair, kind faded blue eyes. He smiled genially at Jennie when introduced.

"I see you're running a hospital annex here," he smiled, the wrinkles folding naturally as if he did it often.

"We hope it's only colds, but we don't dare take a chance with Ruth," Caroline answered, leading him to the sick bay.

Dave hurried in, dripping from a quick sluicing at the outside pump. "Wyatt told me to work by the barn so I could see when Doc arrived," he said, accepting the towel from Jennie with a nod of thanks.

So Big Brother could be kind. Why should she be surprised? Where his family was concerned, his benevolent consideration was assured.

Suddenly she felt terribly lonely. Would she always be looking in from the outside on a warm family unit? How wonderful it would be to have the aura of protection, the comfort of someone placing her number one in his heart.

There was work to be done, and she turned resolutely from her thoughts. She moved swiftly, banishing the uncomfortable longing. A writer's life by necessity was a lonely one, she reminded herself fiercely. She had always been proud of her self-containment. Why this vacillating now that she had a modicum of success?

"It's no use sending her to the hospital," she heard the doctor tell Dave. "Knowing that little mother, she would fret over leaving the children behind. She's entering the last trimester of her pregnancy and so long as we keep her coughing under control, she should manage all right. However, do call her obstetrician. He won't make house calls, but I will be only too happy to talk with him."

They hurried to the library to telephone.

Jennie was stirring the Beef Stroganoff when Wyatt and Fred returned from their chores, and met the two coming from the library.

The low rumble of male voices came to her as they discussed the next move, but Jennie remained by the stove, keeping her back to them. She poured a large measure of wine into the simmering beef. *I hope Wyatt gets drunk on it,* she thought defiantly. Then perversely, a smile twitched her lips upon imagining the lurching figure of the high and mighty elder brother. No such luck. He no doubt had two hollow legs.

The doctor made appreciative remarks over the aromas from the stove and was promptly invited to dinner. It fell upon Caroline to entertain him while the men showered.

Poor Caroline. Wyatt, the Overlord, would be expecting her to cancel her trip. Jennie sighed.

Dave carried the trays to the sickrooms, then made Jennie join them for the predinner cocktail.

"You're a brick pitching in like this," he said warmly, his hand on her back as he led her to the others. "Even Ruth said she feels better, knowing you are here."

She smiled up at him. "I'm really enjoying it," she confessed. "My kitchen has the usual basic room, but this one gives me all the space I need. I love cooking, but it's no fun doing it for myself. I love having appreciative eaters."

Wyatt was with the doctor by the fireplace. Caroline was not there. She must have grabbed the opportunity to speak to Fred. How quickly could she convince her husband to concur with her plans?

When the two returned, Jennie was immediately aware of the tension between them. Caroline's eyes were bright with unshed tears, while Fred's mouth was in the tight controlled line his brother maintained.

Poor Caroline! It looked as though there would be no trip after all.

Wyatt's gaze kept going to them during dinner. The Ever-Watchful Protector. At least he was too concerned about them to notice her.

They smiled in anticipation when Jennie brought in her chocolate cake. Standing at the sideboard, she cut thick moist slices.

"Jennie is interested in climbing our little butte," Caroline said, passing the filled plates. "I warned her not to try it by herself. But knowing my cousin, I'm advising you to show her the way, Wyatt, before she does it."

Jennie stared at her in angry surprise. What was she doing? She was well aware of the antagonism between them.

He must have seen her reaction, but his face was a blank mask. "I'll see if I can make the time. It should be done before the winds start their winter blast."

"It's not necessary," she said tensely. "I'm too busy in the kitchen."

Caroline hooted. "You have prepared enough in the refrigerator for several days. Why don't you go tomorrow, Wyatt? The weather forecast promises a good day, and I've heard how it can blow once winter sets in."

"Has your cousin ever done any climbing? It shouldn't be tried with city muscles."

Their eyes met, his coolly disdainful, hers hotly rebellious.

"Look at her," Caroline said. "Does she look like she's soft?"

Male eyes examined her, impaling her as she stood by the sideboard.

"In the right places," Fred said with a grin.

Caroline rumpled his hair as she handed him his plate. The tenseness which had been between the two suddenly dissolved under the general laughter.

"Down, boys," she laughed. "I mean, when not writing, our Jennie is a sports fiend. Her tennis would lay you low."

"She deserves a break from kitchen duty," Fred inserted.

Wyatt looked at her from hooded eyes. "If the weather stays promising, would you like to make the attempt?" he asked.

Jennie was about to decline, then abruptly nodded agreement. He would dearly love to have her back off, but she really would like to attempt the climb. City muscles, indeed!

The bomb came as they had coffee. The doctor had just finished telling an amusing story, when Wyatt looked down the table.

"Which reminds me, did you remember to cancel your plane reservations, Cary? I'm sorry your jaunt has to be cancelled but you girls should be able to make it next week."

Caroline's gaze went imploringly to her

husband. He gave her a strange look of reluctant resignation and turned to his brother.

"We were talking about it. When I heard about the proposed trip, I made arrangements with a wholesaler in Dallas for Cary to pick up supplies for my jewelry. She has to go now because he's going out of business and it's cash and carry with up to fifty percent off."

Wyatt raised an eyebrow. "The cost of the trip would negate any profit," he observed.

"True, but he has things which are hard to find," Fred continued doggedly. "I don't know where I can get them otherwise, and I have to replenish my stock."

Poor Fred, Jennie thought, commiserating with him.

"Besides, I want to go," Caroline added defiantly. "I'm very interested in Fred's work and want to learn more about it."

Wyatt's eyes were shuttered, but Jennie knew he was adding and subtracting.

"And what about our Cordon Bleu cook," he asked sarcastically, "is she leaving too?"

"I wouldn't leave you in this crisis," Jennie said hurriedly, then blushed. That sounded as though Caroline were unfeeling about leaving them now.

Later, Caroline thanked Jennie for championing her cause. Though she didn't mention it, Jennie was conscious of a thread of resentment in her own thoughts. What right did the

Mighty King have to try to regulate her cousin's life as if she were a child?

She carried the anger to bed with her, to
carefully nurture the resentment as a fence
against him. Her eyes blinked open. Why did
she think she needed protection?

Chapter Six

The sky was barely light when the loud
bleating from the sheep woke her. She was
instantly alert, fearful something was wrong.
She leaned far out the window, her breath
coming out in thick clouds in the cold air.

She could barely make out the huddled
sheep being urged into waiting carriers. The
long aluminum sides of the trailer-trucks sat
like silvery ghosts in the predawn light. Wyatt
had said they were loading in the morning,
but this early?

She nudged the thermostat as she hurried
to the kitchen. The men would need a substantial breakfast to withstand this cold. She
was too late. Three cups sat on the table with
a jar of instant coffee.

She peered out the kitchen door, to be forced
back by the cold. Shivering, she put on the
coffeepot. The men would be back around ten
for breakfast. She went to work. She hauled in
the two double gallon Thermos jugs in which
they carried water on the work truck. One was

filled with hot coffee, strong and laced with a small amount of brandy. Into the other went her chicken soup, boiling hot. No one should work on an empty stomach in this freezing weather, she reasoned.

She put on an old quilted jacket and tied a woolen scarf around her head. Then she brought up Caroline's little Fiat and loaded the car along with every mug on the shelves. She didn't know if the Mighty Wyatt would approve, but she bet the other men would welcome this largess.

The trailers were huge double-deckers. Besides the brothers, there were the truck drivers two Basques with their four dogs. The dogs contained the sheep, but cajoling them up the incline into the dark mouth of the truck sometimes took brute force.

Fred was the closest and she brought two steaming mugs to him.

"Coffee or soup?" she asked brightly.

His face was red from the wind, and he let out a whoop upon seeing her offering. He stripped off a glove and gratefully wrapped a cold hand around the hot cup.

"I didn't know we had angels in this section of the state! Hey, fellows, look what has dropped down from heaven!"

They crowded around her, and she watched anxiously as the hot contents were downed, wondering why their mouths weren't scalded.

"Wowie! What did you put in the coffee!" one truck driver exclaimed.

Wyatt handed her his cup for a refill and she looked at him with apprehension. "It was only a little brandy," she confessed. "It was all right, wasn't it?"

White teeth flashed in a smile. "Very all right," he said. "We were all feeling the cold. This wind makes it murder."

His hands went up and tugged the scarf back on her head. It had slid off while she had been busy filling cups. "Can't have you get a chill, can we," he murmured. "You've become an important part of the family."

Startled, she stared up at him, his mug clasped in her hands. The sun was peeping over the horizon, casting him in bronze. His hands went over hers to slowly retrieve his coffee.

Dave came over requesting soup, and the spell was broken.

"When will you be ready for breakfast?" she asked, not daring to look at him when she returned his cup.

Wyatt squinted toward the trucks where the work was back in progress. "They're moving well. Between nine and ten. Still want to climb the butte?"

Jennie nodded. "If you're not too tired," she amended.

"Fix a lunch. Something I can carry in a

backpack," he ordered, then swung back to the trucks.

"Dress in layers," Wyatt advised when she finished making sandwiches and filled a Thermos bottle with coffee. "A sweater, a heavier cardigan, and a windbreaker. If it warms up, you can peel off to stay comfortable."

A nylon windbreaker was borrowed from Ruth, and they took off in the truck. The road was in the same rutted condition as that first fateful one she took into the Dubrow Ranch and she clung valiantly to her seat.

"After this," she said as he slowed to navigate a deep pothole, "climbing that hill should be a pushover."

He grinned as he pressed the accelerator. "I have full confidence in you. You're made of sterner material than your cousin."

Close to the base, the butte loomed alarmingly in the perpendicular, sending qualms through her. What had she let herself in for?

"Have you ever done this before?" he asked, adjusting the backpack that carried their lunch.

"Nothing this steep," she admitted.

He pointed to the trail they would follow, showing how it switched back and forth on its way to the top.

"It's faint but the handholds are there.

There's only one section we have to be careful with. See that brown strata near the top? That rock crumbles and can't be depended upon. Fortunately we were able to build the path at a more gradual slope so there shouldn't be any trouble."

"You made the trail?" she asked, incredulous.

"Can you imagine three hellions growing up with this challenge without finding a way to the top?" he grinned. "Many an Indian fight was fought up there. It's a great place from which to send smoke signals."

Jennie had a sudden vision of a dark-haired boy scrambling up the steep incline to surprise his younger brothers.

Wyatt was watching her quizzically as she hurried to catch up to him.

A third of the way up, Jennie experienced the first cramp in her calf. Upon his insistence, she was leading the way. He did not want any dislodged stones falling on her.

She braced against the wall as she massaged the offending leg. "Sorry about this," she said ruefully. "Evidently tennis uses different muscles.'

"I can get at it better," he said, kneeling on the narrow ledge and kneading with strong fingers.

His head was bent by her waist, and the need to touch the vibrant hair was overpowering. Gently, she laid a tentative finger on a strand. Did his hands falter a second? No, he could never have felt that light touch. Her heart was beating heavily in her rib cage.

"It's better now," she said, her voice unsteady.

He rose beside her, blocking her vision. "We're not to the point of no return," he said, gazing down at her with a curiously closed look. "We can still turn back."

And escape? Mentally she shook herself. There was no reason to read a double entendre in his suggestion.

"You're not going to call me a quitter, Wyatt Dubrow." her laugh was a little breathless.

His eyes crinkled with amusement, "It never would have occurred to me to do so," he replied, helping her over the rocks that crumbled at her feet.

He made her stop to rest before crossing the soft rock area. The ledge was wide enough for them to sit hunched down next to each other.

"Thanks for stopping," she gasped. "I didn't want to suggest it in case you were after some speed record."

He cocked his head to look at her. "Crazy kid! I was beginning to think you part mountain goat."

They exchanged a warm companionable grin. This was better. No lurching heartbeat, only easy rapport over the satisfaction from shared exercise, a matched enjoyment over meeting a physical challenge.

Her gaze went over the scene below. "My, it goes on forever!" she said with awe. "It's different from seeing it from an airplane."

"Yes," he agreed, flipping a stone over the precipice. "Wait until you get the complete panoramic view."

"Then let's hurry. I'm getting hungry."

He vaulted the last three feet and held his hands to help her over the ledge. The wind tore at them and he led her from the edge. Then with his arm protectively around her waist, she took in the full view from the flat top.

It was a harsh land, a bleak land, but she could imagine not hostile to one who understood its beauty.

"Oh, Wyatt!" It came out as a sigh of reverence.

"You feel it, don't you," he murmured.

She turned in the circle of his arm to smile up at him, her eyes luminous. And there, with the wind tugging at their clothes, she was enclosed in his arms.

He released her, and they stared wordlessly at each other, a guarded question in both their eyes. He put out his hand, and she placed hers unhesitatingly in it.

The top measured less than an acre. He led her around, pointing to landmarks, telling some of the known history of the places.

He finally settled her behind a boulder as protection from the unrelenting wind, then opened the knapsack. They ate heartily of the thick roast beef sandwiches. She peeled an egg for him as he poured the steaming coffee. They sat with their backs against the boulder, munching on crisp apples.

"Now you know why I don't relocate where the pasture is more lush," he said. "There are a few of us strange creatures who don't want to see their neighbors, who don't have to socialize every day. I'd smother if I saw another house from my front door. I guess you could accuse me of being a recluse."

She gave an understanding smile. "You're almost as bad as I am when my writing takes hold. I resent interruptions and frequently wish I were on a desert island."

"What do you want out of life, Jennie?" he asked.

The question startled her. Her writing, was her first thought, then she hesitated. Was it the beginning and end of her desires?

"That's an odd question," she said thoughtfully. "My writing is important to me, naturally. But I don't know if it will always be enough. I guess, like most women, eventually a husband to love, and a raft of kids."

"What an ambitious program!" he mocked.

"Which, the husband to love, or the raft of children?" she asked.

He gazed down on her, smiling. "Oh, you'll find the husband, all right. It's the number of children I'm thinking about."

Her smile matched his. "I guess I could cut down on the number but I thought men liked children. Don't you?"

He rubbed his jaw in reflection. "Yes, I'd like several. I would want a son. Most men would. But I would like a daughter also. If I should marry the woman I loved, I would want to return a duplicate to the world for some future man to find happiness with."

The concept astonded her. Is that how he would feel about his wife? The idea shook her, and she gathered the remnants of their lunch to stuff them in the knapsack.

"Now that we've repopulated the world, we better head back," she said brightly. "If I sit much longer, my muscles will refuse to budge."

This time he led. "If you slip, I'll try to stop you," he explained.

"Don't say try," she said dryly. "Promise to make an all-out effort!"

He chuckled as she hung feet first over the edge until he guided her to the first ledge, a short drop below. "You can stand now," he assured her. "I have to protect you. Think of all those future progeny depending upon you!"

The descent was accomplished with the minimum of sliding, and they rattled home over the rough road.

"A hot bath is first on my agenda," she groaned as she stumbled off the high step of the truck. "You win. I do have soft muscles."

He steadied her, laughing. "But all in the right places, as Fred so aptly stated."

She grinned up at him, only to let it fade under the intense stare from yellow eyes.

"I had a very enjoyable time, Jennie," he said softly.

She gave a slight nod, unable to speak. His mouth came down in a swift hard kiss.

He flicked the tip of her nose before jumping back into the truck to drive it to the barn. She walked blindly into the house, her fingers pressed on her lips.

No, she said feebly. No. But her scattered wits didn't tell her what she was protesting against.

She waited expectantly after dinner. What would be his next move when the family gathered as usual in the living room?

The answer came quickly. Dave left to be with his wife. Fred moved around restlessly for a while, then excused himself, saying he had a design he was anxious to get down on paper before he forgot it. Wyatt rose and her pulse quickened.

"It's been a long day for all of us," he said without preamble. "I know you want to get to bed, and I have some paper work to get out of the way before I can do likewise. Good-night, Jennie."

She stared after him, shocked by the abrupt leave-taking. He acted as though he couldn't get away from her fast enough.

So that was that. She had thought he had shared the special awareness of the afternoon, but it had all been in her imagination. Her face burned, recalling her flights of fancy after that last swift kiss, the unexpected tenderness she thought she saw in his glance.

It was gone. Over. As if it never had been.

Chapter Seven

The next morning Jennie brought Ruth her breakfast.

"I seem to be sleeping my life away," Ruth said weakly, taking the glass of fresh juice Jennie held for her.

"Best way to get over the bug," Jennie reassured her. "I hear your temperature is down, so you're over the worse part."

"But I feel like such a burden," she said petulantly.

"A care, yes. Burden, no," Jennie returned easily. "It's your two monsters, who are coming out of it, who will be tearing the place apart."

"No more than usual," Rugh said with resignation. "Now that we've taken over this sitting room as our bedroom, they've lost their play area. Their activities are confined to their room."

Jennie returned to her chair, and took in the cluttered room. "You should have a home of your own now that you're expanding your family."

Ruth gave a wistful smile, very similar to Caroline's when the subject had been mentioned.

"I would dearly love one," she admitted with a sigh. "When first married, Dave and I even picked out a spot on the other side of the stream. He did mention it to Wyatt, but he said there were these unused rooms available." she picked nervously at the coverlet. "At the time he was right, but we seem to be so productive . . ." she added, managing a rueful smile.

Indignation flared again. The Omnipotent Dictator! So busy directing lives! Couldn't he ever let go of the reins?

"Don't you think it's time you made your wishes known?" she said heatedly. "Both you and Caroline want your own homes. I think it's sinful the way you bow down to one man's direction. He's downright cruel!"

"Oh, no, he's nothing like that!" Ruth protested. "You don't understand. Dave owes Wyatt so much that he does't want to hurt him. He gave up his own hope for a family after their parents died. If we can fill in for that loss in some small way, we will."

"He's not that ancient," Jennie pointed out with sarcasm. "He still can produce his own loyal following. Surely there are women in his life!"

Ruth gave a light laugh. "Of course! Wyatt is considered open season by every unattached female in the area. But there has been no hint of anything serious except for Lorraine, and that was ten years ago."

There was that name again. Lorraine, the woman who had jilted him when he had needed her, the woman who had scarred him so that he could never again love another enough to marry. Sight unseen, she hated her.

"That still is no reason why you shouldn't have your own home," Jennie continued firmly. "You said you wanted to build on this land. It isn't as if you would be miles away."

Ruth gazed at her thoughtfully. "You know, you're right! We accepted his desire in the beginning, then drifted into this impasse. Things are different now that our family has grown. I wonder if I can convince Dave we should bring up the subject again!"

Jennie smothered her smile of relief. The seed was planted. Maybe if the two families approached him with a united appeal, the Grand Patriarch would cut the umbilical cord. There was some hope for her cousin.

"I know Caroline feels the same need," she said casually. "Fred, of course, feels bound by the same commitment as Dave, but if you approach him together, Wyatt will have to see reason."

She gazed down at her clenched hands.

Why did she feel like the snake sliding into Eden, offering a bite from the Forbidden Fruit? Wyatt did not rate her loyalty. He had proven he was only able to be considerate to her when he felt obligated. The first time was the plane ride after she offered to do kitchen duty, the second was a reluctant agreement to show her the butte when she continued after Caroline left.

She refused to recall the different man he had been on those trips. The real man was here, caustic, domineering, belittling, ready to stab her with subtle words whenever she acted normally friendly to his brothers. His unhealthy possessiveness of his family had proved to her how impossible he was.

He had only been charming on those other occasions to win Jennie over to his point of view—to use her. Well, she would be on guard from now on. Her greatest joy would come when she had extricated Wyatt's younger brothers from his ridiculous stranglehold. She renewed her efforts to persuade Ruth to take a stand.

"Do you think it might work?" Ruth asked faintly, her doubts showing.

"Talk it over with your husband," Jennie said sharply. "I can't understand this reluctance you women show. You have your life to live and it can't always be in the shadow of a brother who ignores the fact you might want a life of your own. How long will you subjugate yourself because he did what he *wanted* to do ten years ago? It isn't as if you're going off and leaving him! You are only asking for what any married couple wants, a home of your own!"

How did she get on this soapbox? She had never been this vindictive toward anyone before. If Wyatt ever found out she was behind this, he would be furious!

"Look," she said, suddenly anxious to soft-peddle her vehemence. "It's only a suggestion. Please don't even tell your husband we talked about it."

The men were sitting around the fireplace when she joined them for the predinner cocktail. They were discussing evidence of rustling found on one section of Franjule's ranch.

"How do they get away with it?" Jennie asked

"They do it mainly at night," Wyatt angrily explained. "It is no more the old-fashioned roundup and sneaking them to market. They come now with a refrigerator truck and butchers. The animals are slaughtered, dressed and packed ready for the stores, and are gone by daylight.

"A good butcher can dress down a sheep in five to fifteen minutes. You can see how fast they can go through a flock. Then the next day all we have are the buzzards to alert us to where they had worked."

"How terrible!" she exclaimed.

"Yes," Dave added bitterly. "They can overnight wipe out a year's profit."

"Is there no way to protect yourselves?" she
asked.

"With all this territory to monitor?" he re-
buked. "We were doing night patrols by air.
It's the only way to check. They need lights to
do their work, and that can be spotted from
the air."

"Have any been captured?"

"Yes, But as quickly as one is caught and
we relax a little, another is formed. With the
soaring price of meat, it makes the risk worth-
while."

Jennie's glance was guilty at the man by the
fireplace. He was nursing his drink, the fur-
rows deep on his face. He had enough problems without her stirring up any at the home
front!

Fred was staring out the window and she
moved casually to stand next to him.

"Hear anything from Caroline?" she asked.

"No," he answered. "I don't expect to either
until she's finished and ready to fly back. You
knew she was going to San Francisco also?"

"Yes, she mentioned it. Oh, Fred, I hope
she's successful for both of your sakes!"

He turned worried eyes to her, brown eyes
with only scratches of yellow. "That could
open a Pandora's box. Once opened, we might
not like what it reveals."

At that moment he was not concerned about

himself, she sensed, but the effect on his brother.

Such misplaced devotion! she fumed. Big Brother was well able to stand alone. If not, it was time for him to learn!

"How did your design go last night?" she probed.

His face lit up. "I can't wait to start on it. It's three-dimensional and the concept was haunting me, and how to execute it. Then, while in the barn, everything fell into place. Would you like to see it?" he asked eagerly.

"I have five minutes before I have to go back to the kitchen," she answered. "Let's go."

Wyatt was quiet through most of the dinner. He was obviously worried about the rustling.

Fred, after exhausting the topic of his new design, grew quiet too, no doubt mulling over the future and how to approach his brother when Caroline returned.

Jennie wondered why she had bothered with the elaborate chicken pot pie with the three inch puff pastry. After their first smile of anticipation, they ate with no further comment. Tomorrow, she vowed, they would get leftovers. She was beginning to resent the time spent in the kitchen even though the work helped assuage her ricocheting emotions.

Tomorrow she would go for a long walk and

use some of this nervous energy. The butte was little over a mile away, and she wondered if she dared climb it by herself.

"Are there any interesting sights within walking distance?" she asked, breaking into the silence. "I would like to see some of the area more closely. Who knows, I might use your ranch as background in some future novel!"

"Do you ride?" Fred asked. "That's the best way to cover the area and be able to see it."

"A little," she admitted. "I don't have much opportunity in Chicago," she added wryly.

"How about trying it tomorrow? I could take you to an area where I find most of the stones I use in my necklaces."

Jennie leaned forward eagerly. "That would be fun."

"I'll take her," Wyatt cut in. "We spoke this morning about Devil needing more exercise. Pedro hasn't been around to handle him while I was busy. We don't want to lose the ground we've gained with him."

"Devil!" she cried aghast, recalling the huge beast as he had reared in front of her car. What was he trying to do, kill her?

"We have a quiet horse for you," Wyatt advised her, his lips twitching. He turned to Fred. "You'd better concentrate on getting Jennie's car fixed. You're the mechanic in the family."

Fred gave a faint shrug. "Okay, but if you

find any interesting stones, be sure to bring them back to me. My selection is getting limited. It was too hot this summer to go to Bailey's *Arroyo*."

"Bailey was an old prospector Dad let live out his last years on our ranch," Wyatt broke in. "We'd take him some tobacco and provisions whenever we were in the area. I'll tell you more about him when we get going."

Jennie's first inclination was to make an excuse for not going, but now her curiosity was aroused. If she could find some stones for Fred, so much the better.

The day dawned crisply clear. The heat of those first days was over but it promised to be warm by noon. Jennie couldn't hide her apprehension when Wyatt roped the black horse. The powerful beast snorted and pranced before suffering the bridle. Was she supposed to ride beside this brute? Devil was his name, and the devil showed in rolling eyes and bared teeth.

She breathed a sigh of relief upon seeing the docile pinto Fred was saddling for her.

"If I can't move when I return," she said dolefully once seated on its wide back, "dinner is in the yellow casserole dish. Put it in the oven at 350 until it bubbles."

"We've got a good horse liniment that will put fire to sore muscles," Dave grinned.

"Right now I think it should be rubbed on

my head for attempting this. Ignore me if I come up with anymore bright ideas. I'm still aching from the climb yesterday."

"I can bet," Fred said mercilessly. "You'll be using a whole different set of muscles today. We'll take turns rubbing you."

"I can hardly wait!" she returned dourly "Your kindness overwhelms me. Lead on, Wyatt Dubrow, before I reconsider. The torture, I know, begins tomorrow."

They rode off amid the laughter. Wyatt eyed her critically as he held them to a sedate walk.

"Getting the feel of it?" he asked finally.

She nodded, settling into the movement of the horse. How long ago was it since she had cantered safely around the sheltered park in Chicago? How different was this vastness before her!

"Baldy should give you no trouble," Wyatt said, his knuckles white as he fought the dancing of his horse. "See the cleft in the hills ahead? Head for there. I have to let Devil have his run to use up some of this energy. I'll be waiting for you."

She waved him on, marveling at the control he had over the beast. The stallion was bigger than any she had ever seen, and his restlessness was making her horse uneasy. She was glad to see them take off, leaving a trail of dust. Soon the land and the sky were hers.

She urged the horse on and he moved in an easy loping canter that she soon fell in with.

Wonderful! She might have to pay for this later, but now it was pure enjoyment.

The gray sagebrush was more prominent now, fighting for place with the range grass. Would Wyatt have to burn here to prevent it from ruining this pastureland? What constant problems he must face, from fluctuating market prices, to worry if the scant rain would be enough to nourish this parched land another season. There had been talk of marauding coyotes and of the increase in rustling. With all these problems, perhaps she had been wrong to stir the brothers into rebellion. Surely in his home he should have peace.

A deep dense of guilt inundated her. What right did she, an outsider, have to disrupt their life-style! If they were dissatisfied, they should seek their own solution. Caroline would have to manage without any more of her help.

It was getting warmer and she zipped open her jacket. There was no trace of Wyatt. He had run his horse in wide arcs until they had both disappeared in the vee formed between the hills.

A plume of smoke caught her eye. It was a dust devil. She watched it idly as it swirled, moving with surprising speed until it left its contact with the ground. It vanished as if in a cloud of smoke. Miniature tornadoes, Wyatt had called them.

She neared the hills and Wyatt came toward

her, Devil now running at an easy gallop, a white lather spraying from his coat.

"Is he behaving better?" she asked as he pulled up.

"Yes. He has to get that first run out of his system, then he quiets down. There's some water in the basin ahead. We'll give them a breather there."

Devil was definitely better behaved. He even shortened his long stride to accomodate poor Baldy. A group of cottonwood trees announced the water hole and they stopped in the shade.

Jennie clung to him with embarrassment when he assisted her down.

"I have no legs!" she cried, "I'll never make it back!"

"You need to walk," he grinned, supporting her. "Come on, make those legs move. You'll feel better when they loosen."

She held on longer than necessary. The breeze brought the fragrance of sagebrush with, blended with the man and horse scent, made her head swim.

"Do we have much further to go?" she asked.

She surprised a look of sympathy in his eyes. "We'll only go as far as you want. The Bailey place we spoke about is another two miles. There's a little valley beyond these hills. Spring rains have cut a narrow gorge through it, and that is where Fred finds those streaked stones he likes to polish. They say part of this area used to be ocean, and stones are smooth like those you find on beaches. We also find occasional semiprecious ones which have washed down from the mountains."

"Like our garnet?" she asked.

His eyes flickered. "Like our garnet."

"I don't know how much bending I'll be able to do but let's give it the old college try," she said with a grin. Maybe she would find just the stone Fred was looking for, a stone that would inspire him to create a special master-piece.

The valley was no more than a half dozen miles long, bisected by the gash they called Bailey's *Arroyo*. Here there was no grass and little sagebrush. The cacti were the only vege-tation able to survive this near desert. The high hills deflected even the minimum rain received elsewhere.

"One of the most beautiful sights I've ever seen was here," he said surprisingly. "I came shortly after a vagrant rainstorm and the ground was covered with pink and yellow flowers."

The wind whipped dust at them as Jennie gazed over the barren landscape. "I'll have to take your word for it because I've only read of such occurrences. Is this where Bailey lived? How could he exist without water?"

"He had a windmill. This land is criss-crossed with underland streams. Most are salty, a heritage of the ancient ocean, but he had a fresh one. He irrigated a small plot of land and lived there with only a burro for company." He pointed to a gray blur. "That's Bailey's shack. Want to check it out?"

As they got closer Jennie looked in amazement at the withered branches from the dried cottonwood trees surrounding the small, weather-beaten shack. Now that the broken window no longer worked, all vegetation was dead. It seemed impossible that anyone had been able to survive in such a barren landscape.

"It's so dry that nothing rots," Wyatt explained, assisting Jennie again from her horse. "It looks much the same as the last time I was here."

The door sagged open and Jennie peered inside. A cot with a thin, broken mattress, a homemade table with one chair and a potbellied stove was the complete inventory. What drove a man to live out his life in such stringent quarters?

"He was a strange person," Wyatt said, seemingly aware of her unspoken question. "He talked a blue streak when we dropped by, but he was glad to see us go. Old Bailey was like that. When in town to put together another stake, he was a regular hellion. He wore the girls out," he added with a grin. "Yet once in the desert, he was content to be alone for a year or two at a time."

The wind was increasing as they stepped into the hut. Dust streamers slipped through the cracks between the parched boards.

"How do we get down that cut to search for stones?" Jennie asked, when the wind had somewhat abated,. The sides had looked alarmingly perpendicular.

"A little further along the side has caved in, giving an easier approach," he explained. "It's still a scramble. Think you can do it?"

"Try me!" she called, already out of the cobwebby hovel.

With some sliding on her rear, they made it, laughing over her awkward descent.

"I don't know how I get into these situations," she grinned.

"I will say you're different from most girls I've encountered," he admitted, helping her slap the dust off her jeans.

"And you're the only man who has taken me to such highs and lows," she teased. "How deep is this place?"

They stared up the steep sides. "About fifteen feet," he guessed. "And I hope I don't cause you to go any lower," he added, a twinkle showing in his eyes. "I usually specialize in highs."

She glanced at him with amusement. "I can well imagine. That's a bachelor's privilege."

Jennie moved along the dry stream bed, needing distance to cancel the sudden upbeat of her heart. She better cool things before he thought her flirting and responded to the challenge. She did not want the feel of his lips now, only to be castigated for some ungodly reason later.

She was disappointed by the dull stones until he dampened one from the canteen to show how the variegated veins came up.

"The interesting ones are not here for the shoveling," he said. "It's hunt and choose. Sometimes Fred finds only a half dozen potentially good ones, other times he comes laden with a full knapsack."

She kept two flat oval stones that appealed to her, then started the awkward climb to the top.

"I'm begging off," she said, grunting as her foot slipped and he made a grab for her. "It's too cold down there. That's summer work."

"Then it's an oven. There is no happy medium," he explained.

No wonder Caroline wasn't eager to explore with Fred. Her feet were used to even cement sidewalks. Her adventurous spirit was directed toward the discovery of the best bargain in the next store.

The horses were waiting patiently in the partial shade of the shack. Small dust puffs rose with each step.

"Kee-rist!" the word exploded from him.

Jennie followed his startled gaze, to see a

tall brown column at the far end of the valley. It writhed as it grew in size. Then she realized it was moving rapidly toward them.

A dust devil! But of gigantic size! The same principle of a tornado was inherent in them, and this one was past the playful stage. It came racing at an astonishing speed, picking up debris in whirlwind hands, and flinging it aside.

Wyatt moved quickly. In no time he was by the nervous horses and had quickly led them into the hut.

He came to the door to see Jennie still unmoving, hypnotized by the roaring approach.

"Get over here!" he yelled, running toward her to hurry her.

She started for the pitiful protection of the sagging hut but she was too late. Wyatt tossed her quickly to the ground next to the wall, and lay on top of her. She struggled, startled by his action.

"Stop it!" he ordered as he pulled his open jacket up to cover both their heads.

"I can't breathe—" she cried. She didn't know whether to blame it on the covering jacket or the sensation of his body heavy on her.

"You may never breathe again, if your lungs get full of that dust," he answered curtly.

Now she understood what he was doing, and lay still. The jacket was tented over their heads as protection from the scouring grit-filled wind.

The mini-tornado howled about them but Jennie was only aware of the weight of his body on hers, the heavy beat of his heart against her breast. One hand rested alongside her face, and she recalled in photo detail the dream she had by the little stream. She moved her head a fraction to rub against his cheek.

Then his lips were on hers, and the kiss became part of the screaming wind as it grabbed at their legs, twisting at their clothes. Something primitive rose in her, fed by the basic elements unleashed around them.

She was pressed hard against the ground as he counteracted the pull of the wind, and her body arched against him in a language of its own. The thunder of their heartbeats was part of the banshee wail around them, the unharnessed demanding hunger of the kiss an answer to the savage thrust of the wind.

It was a wild, unnerving experience, and the wrenching crash as the roof was lifted from the building was part of the tumult tearing through her.

As fast as it had developed, it was gone. When reaching the *arroyo*, it lost its energy, a trail of boards from the hut's roof showing its path.

"Remind me to invite you to the next sandstorm," Wyatt said with a twisted grin as he helped her up. "You are much softer than the ground and have other, er, attractions."

"I'll keep it in mind," she said dryly, seemingly concentrating on brushing at the dust. She needed time to regain control of her emotions.

Keep it light, girl, keep it light, she warned herself. He mustn't see how his kisses had devastated her.

"I will say you go all out to entertain guests, but a little less dramatics, please. I was fascinated by your dust devils, but you can keep those large economy-sized ones!"

And kisses that sear, but mean nothing to you, she added to herself as the clamor in her slowly subsided. How could he act so untouched by what had just happened!

"What on earth?" Fred exploded when they rode into the corral. "What did you do, roll her down the *arroyo*?"

"No, we met a dust devil that was bigger than us," Wyatt answered, his hands remaining on her waist after helping her from Baldy.

Fred was beside her, his hand on her arm in consternation. "You run in and soak in the hottest water you can stand," he ordered. "I'll take care of Baldy for you."

Jennie experienced an odd swirl of vertigo. Both men were too close. Strange electric currents snapped between them. Their broad shoulders were blocking all air, and she was breathing deeply, craving oxygen.

Then she was standing alone, swaying slightly. The two men stepped back, and she wondered at the withdrawn expressions on their faces.

"Thanks, Fred," she said with a shaky voice, drawing a hand through gritty hair. "And I promise to clean the tub for you, Wyatt, like a good guest. You need a shower as much as I do."

She managed a light laugh, looking at his streaked face. "We must look as though we had indulged in a dust war."

A light gleamed bright in yellow eyes as a finger brushed her cheek. "I'll war with you anytime you want," he murmured, sending a hot flush racing to her face. So he had't been immune, only more in control. Thank goodness, because it wouldn't have taken much for her to remain in his arms, demanding more.

They turned in surprise as a small red car came down the lane, a long dust trail showing its speedy progress.

"Well, I'll be—it's Lorraine!" Fred exclaimed as the door opened and a woman stepped out.

The man beside her stiffened and an icy hand closed around Jennie's heart.

"This is a surprise, Lorraine!" Fred cried, going to the woman with hand outstretched. "We haven't seen you in years. When did you come home?"

The Franjules were Basques and Spanish

blood was evident in the dark good looks of this woman. She had pulled back her hair in a smart chignon and unbuttoned her blouse to its last button revealing her well rounded breasts. Her black eyes snapped in anticipation.

"Fred, you look wonderful! I hear you're married to a dream of a girl. How nice for you!" she said, raising her cheek for his kiss. "I hope you have more luck than I had. Tom and I have finally called it quits." Her eyes were on Wyatt still standing by Jennie.

Wyatt's face was expressionless. Remembering his control, Jennie wondered how the news was being digested; was he happy that Lorraine was again available? Was he enjoying this display of her ripe charms?

Lorraine swept up to Wyatt, fluttering her long lashes. She raised her lips expectantly, full, red, pulsing with promise.

Jennie winced as Wyatt's mouth brushed hers.

"I'm surprised too, Lorraine," he said. "When I spoke to your father last week, he didn't mention you were expected home."

Her body moved seductively against him as she smiled, arching her neck to look up at him all too well aware of the effect of her blouse buttoned extra low.

"I told him not to spread the word," Lorraine said, placing a hand on his upper arm, letting fingers knead lightly into strong biceps. "I wanted to surprise everyone. You're the first to know. I persuaded mom that I wasn't in mourning, and talked them into a party Saturday for their newly unattached daughter. I'm spreading the good word through the area, but first I wanted to make certain you were free to come. The rest of the family, too, of course," she added hastily.

Wyatt looked at his brother. "Will Caroline be back?"

When Fred nodded, he continued, "Dave will want to stay with Ruth. She's recuperating from the flu."

The woman flicked her hand, dismissing Dave and his problems. "That shouldn't keep you from coming."

Jennie started to move away, fuming over being so impolitely ignored. Wyatt's hand closed over her wrist, pulling her close.

"You haven't met our guest, Jennifer Robbins, Lorraine Franjule from the adjacent ranch. Jennie is Caroline's cousin."

Speculative eyes swept coolly over Jennie's dust-streaked face, disheveled hair and filthy, wrinkled outfit.

"How nice to have the Dubrow ranch available for a vacation," she said sweetly.

"Yes, the Dubrow brothers have been most hospitable," Jennie answered just as sweetly. "If you'll excuse me, I must shower, As you can see, Wyatt and I have been rolling in the dust." She had the satisfaction of seeing Lorraine start, but was annoyed by the quick glint of amusement on Wyatt's face.

Damn that man, he was enjoying the little battle!

Jennie poured bath oil into the water and sank into the tub with a sigh. How every muscle ached! She had been a fool to do so much the past two days. Tomorrow she'd be incapable of movement.

Soaking contentedly, she went over the last two days. Recalling the beauty of the vista from the top of the butte, she knew it was worth it. The heat penetrated her tired muscles while her thoughts drifted dreamily to the man she had shared lunch with on the windy promontory. She felt again the magic of that kiss, so different from the wild one they had indulged in today.

She shifted to the day's happenings, to relive with a disturbing clarity the violent kiss amid the tearing windstorm, and the shared unbridled passion sweeping them. It had been a wild, erotic experience, and she didn't know which had left her more breathless, her response to the man's passion, or the storming of the elements.

It would be best to tread carefully with this elder Dubrow, she cautioned herself. Those highs were too heady, the lows too nerve tearing.

Not that there was any need for further

concern. His Lorraine was back, Lorraine who had jilted him once, but now showed she was willing to take up where they had left off.

She gazed down at her slim figure. She could offer no competition to that experienced, mature woman.

Hastily, she stepped out of the tub to dry herself briskly. What in the world was she thinking of? she berated herself.

Ruth was ensconced on the sofa when Jennie came out of the kitchen to join the family for a cocktail.

Ruth's face was flushed, and her eyes bright, but it did not seem to be from a temperature but from an inner excitement. Dave, in contrast, appeared withdrawn, a frown straining between his brows. Jennie wondered with alarm if they had been talking about a house.

They drank their cocktails in silence for a few minutes. Finally, with a squaring of his shoulders, Dave cleared his throat. "Wyatt," he started slowly, "Ruth and I have been discussing something we'd like you to think about."

Jennie's heart dropped, knowing immediately what was coming next. This was a family crisis and she got up to leave the room.

Ruth's hand came out, stopping her. "Stay, please," she whispered.

Did they think she would prevent an explosion? Hardly likely. The overlord was not known for his reticence.

"Having the family sick made us—me—realize how confined we are in those rooms," Dave continued. "And with another youngster pending, things are getting tighter. It's time we built our own house."

Wyatt showed no reaction. He sat silently, his long legs stretched before him.

"It was wonderful of you to offer the west wing when we were first married," Ruth broke in, leaning forward in her eagerness. "But as Dave said, we are really getting crowded. And we shouldn't inflict another baby on your household, especially with the twins entering the terrible twos."

One eyebrow went up. "Have I ever complained about the youngsters?"

"Of course not!" she answered. "You've been a wonderful uncle to them, but it's time we had our own place."

"You always acted content with the arrangements," he said coolly. "Why the sudden change?"

Ruth looked at Jennie and Wyatt's eyes hardened as he followed her involuntary glance.

Oh, no! Jennie flinched under the icy accusation. It was obvious he blamed her for fanning the unrest.

"It isn't sudden," Dave protested. "We've

discussed it several times. This sickness, as I said, showed us the time has come to think about the move. Besides, every woman deserves her own kitchen."

Jennie rose in determination. "Speaking about kitchens, it's time I checked the stove." She tried to avoid running to its sanctuary as Wyatt's last words came to her.

"We'll talk on the subject later when your family is back on its feet," Wyatt said, closing the subject firmly.

The Dictator! she fumed. The damned Eeudal Lord! What right had he to hold his desires sacrosanct, ignoring their need.

Gone were her vacillating feelings about the man. The strangely haunting excursions with him were banished as she resumed the battle for her cousin. By championing Ruth's cause, Caroline's wishes were more likely to be fulfilled.

Ruth's face was white by the time they finished dessert, and Jennie was certain the emotional letdown contributed to her exhaustion. The question had been asked, but no answer given.

Dave scooped her up in his arms to carry her to bed. Ruth laughingly protested, but the act was one of tender love, bringing a mist to Jennie's eyes.

She had been held possessively in men's arms before, but never with that proprietory love. Would she ever find the man who would love her so completely? She was pushing twenty-five and she once again wondered if her writing were the beginning and end of her desires.

Jennie finished the dishes and went to the living room. Fred was heading towards his wing, Jennie's flat stones in his hand.

"I'll play with these to see what I can come up with," he said, turning the streaked stones experimentally to different angles.

"Then you plan to work in your room," Wyatt said with evident relief. "I'm going out for the evening. Jennie with those aching muscles will be glad to get to bed early."

Jennie flushed. It was obvious he hadn't wanted her to be alone with his brother.

Fred hesitated, the host in him rejecting leaving the guest alone. A Perverse imp in her grasped the obvious rebuttal.

"Don't worry about me," she said politely. "The scullery maid will heed your wish and scamper to bed shortly."

She had the pleasure of seeing the dusky hue rise under Wyatt's tan. They were accepting her labors in the kitchen and were taking off when she had every right to expect their company.

She tried not to act too obviously the martyr as she picked up a magazine and sank resignedly on the sofa.

Her eyes were roundly innocent as she looked up at the glowering man. "Are you going to see Lorraine?" she asked in a saccharine voice. "Do give her my regards and tell her I enjoyed meeting her."

His lips thinned to a tight line while the muscles twitched along his jaw. They would be soft and sensuous again by the time he greeted the woman, she thought with a dull ache. Somehow her dart had backfired.

Fred sat in the chair across from her, amusement showing in brown eyes. "Go on, Wyatt. She was very definite about you visiting tonight. Somehow I don't think time has mellowed that Spanish temper. I'll keep our Jennie entertained."

"I'd like that," said Jennie. Anything to keep her mind off *that man!* She knew if she went to bed now thinking of Wyatt and Lorraine's meeting, she would never get to sleep. "Fred and I haven't had much time to talk about our old Chicago days," she added.

"I agree, sweetheart," Fred said. "Begone, Big Brother. Jennie girl and I have some history to repeat."

Looking irritated, Wyatt stalked out of the room. Shortly afterward, Jennie heard the front door slam and tires squeal as Wyatt raced his car down the driveway.

"I won't ask what that was all about, dear cousin-in-law," Fred drawled with a speculative lift to his brow. "It is enough for me to see our so controlled brother shaken. Those gray eyes of yours can be instruments of torture. It does my heart good to see our Wyatt isn't so self-contained after all. We were all worried about him."

"I'm sure his Lorraine will make certain he doesn't remain self-contained," Jennie rejoined bitterly.

"Ah, yes, Lorraine," he said, leaning back in the chair. His smile showed he had seen through the woman.

So, he had watched her act and hadn't been deceived by the surface picture! Too bad his brother wasn't as observant.

A lethargy crept over her, a need to retreat within herself. "Wyatt was right," she yawned. "All this fresh air and exercise have caught up with me. You go to your workroom. I know you are dying to see what you can come up with."

Fred chuckled as Jennie rose with a groan. "If you can't make it in the morning, we'll understand. One of us will be up with the horse liniment."

She gave him a baleful look. "I wouldn't give your brother the satisfaction of seeing what he's done to me. I'll be there even if I have to cling to the wall for support."

Jennie went to the kitchen, and when she was certain Fred had gone to his rooms, wrapped herself in a sheepskin jacket and went into the cold night. There was a driving restlessness in her now, and she knew it had to be walked off.

Where was the quiet vacation she had hoped for? She had been prepared for a problem with Caroline, but she had not anticipated that she would have one too. And it was all because of that provoking, irritating brother-in-law of Caroline's! From the first meeting he had condemned her and his unreasonable attitude had hurt her pride more than she cared to admit. Did he treat all women this way? Probably not. The voluptuous Lorraine would know exactly how to elicit another response. He was too much a male to ignore the opportunity.

She shivered, wondering if he was arousing the same turmoil in that woman as he had so expertly done in her. Were they taking up where their engagement had ended?

The wind gusted, and she shivered again. She gazed around bleakly before turning back to the house. The silvery beauty of the moonscape went unnoticed.

She lay sleepless until she heard the car return. Against her better judgment, she checked the luminous dial of her clock on the nightstand.

It was only ten-thirty! She was pleasantly surprised. Wyatt back so early? She sighed softly, and fell back on the pillow, a faint smile playing about her lips. Instantly, she fell asleep.

Later that night, she was wakened by her aching muscles. Unable to find a comfortable position, she got stiffly out of her bed and hobbled painfully around her bedroom. Glancing out the window, she glimpsed a yellow patch of light on the ground below. She looked out, her forehead pressed against the cold windowpane. The light came from the library. So Wyatt was still awake.

Her clock registered midnight.

Chapter Eight

The wind was bitingly cold the next morning, howling mournfully around the corners of the house, warning of worse things to come.

"No use asking for penumonia," Wyatt said after a quick exploratory step outside. "We're caught up with the most pressing jobs. I vote we take a day of rest."

"I'm glad Cary isn't flying in today," Fred said as another gust rattled the windows.

"Have you heard from her?" Jennie asked, passing around the ham and cheese omelet.

"Yes. She's postponed her flight and will be in Saturday morning in plenty of time to get glamorous for Lorraine's party." His eyes were warning her not to question about her success.

"Too bad Ruth isn't well enough to go," she said instead. "I'm available for baby-sitting jobs."

Wyatt stared in surprise, his fork halfway to his mouth. "What do you mean," he demanded. "You're going with us."

"Me?" she asked, startled. "She invited the family. You don't need me. I don't know anyone there and you'll want to spend time with your friends. You don't get to see each other, spread out the way you are.'

"You're family," Fred answered with a warm smile. "And the word is out we're harboring a glamorous creature. Out here, every person is a news item. They'd never forgive us if you were't displayed."

"I didn't bring anything dressy," she objected faintly. She wasn't sure she wanted to see the Franjule ranch, and the daughter who would display her prior claim on Wyatt.

"Cary said the two of you always exchanged clothes. She has things in the closet she's never worn," Fred said dismissing that problem with manlike assuredness.

"You can't let me go without a partner," Wyatt added, buttering his toast.

Now she was truly startled. "But I thought you—she—" she floundered. "Who is Lorraine's partner?" she blurted.

She met his mocking glance with bewilderment, but Fred answered. "Knowing her past record, our Lorraine will make certain all eligible bachelors will be present. She'll have plenty dancing attendance on her."

She lowered the omelet pan to soak in the soapy water. Was she being asked along as a date, or as a possible necessary shield if the woman played the other men against him?

139

The men had turned to practical matters.

"Are the trailers still coming for the last shipment tomorrow?" Dave asked.

Wyatt nodded. "Let's hope the wind will have died down."

Breakfast over, everyone quickly dispersed. Fred disappeared in his workroom, Dave went in search of well-needed rest and Wyatt went resolutely to the library.

At ten, she carried trays to everyone with coffee mugs and the last of the cake.

"Sit and relax," Wyatt ordered, as he rose to take the tray from her, "I need a break from these miserable forms."

She took in the haphazard piles of paper. "You mean you can find sense in this mess?" she laughed.

He glanced ruefully at the desk. "At this point I don't know if I've finished a report or not." he admitted.

She shook her head, thinking of her neatly labeled folders of reference material at home.

"Give yourself a break and buy some folders and a cabinet," she said. "Life has enough problems without struggling through that!"

"Our accountant would be happy," he agreed. "I keep promising myself to do it, but never have the time." His eye gleamed a moment as he glanced at her. "I seem to recall Cary saying you were a secretary."

"No way," she protested. "You're not getting

me involved in that hopeless job! I won't be here long enough to make a dent in it."

"It was only a thought," he said, giving an exaggerated sigh. He pulled out a drawer and opened a box, exposing the manila folders. "That's as far as I got," he said sheepishly.

"No, I won't get involved," she repeated firmly, placing her mug on the tray.

"I had no idea what a big business ranching was," she said two hours later.

She was sitting on the carpet, neat stacks of bills and letters spaced around her. They had worked diligently together. Under his direction, she had lined them in proper categories and now only the lettering on the folders was necessary.

"At times it seems so. If only I could claim as steady a profit!"

They had to refer frequently to his ledger which proved up-to-date when seeking where a particular article should be filed. She had noted there were marginal months, but overall a comfortable profit was shown. Wyatt, however was not reaping all the benefit. She was quick to see the monthly checks he gave his brothers. They were generous, far larger than what he gave himself.

This was a side of the man of which she had caught only an occasional glimpse. Did the brothers know the extent of his generosity?

Like many people, his parents had made a

will when the first child had arrived, leaving their estate to the new son and heir. Then when other children came, they never got back to changing that first will.

Upon their death Wyatt was left with a shaky ranch to rescue. It was the only means he had to assure a home for his brothers and sister. He had more than succeeded but supporting three families, plus the ranch hands, at times put a severe strain on him, especially with a fluctuating market.

Now she could better appreciate the respect and obligation the brothers extended to this strong man.

The brass clock chimed the hour, and Jennie looked up in surprise. "Lunchtime!" she exclaimed. "It's back to the kitchen for me!"

A groan escaped as she tried protesting muscles. "You've turned me into an old woman, Wyatt Dubrow!" she moaned accusingly, grimacing as she struggled to rise.

He was beside her, lifting her from her position on the floor.

"You poor kid," he murmured. "You're the one who should be in bed. Never mind lunch, we'll scrounge around."

"And have you eat things I'm saving for later? Never!" she cried, clinging helplessly to his arm while experimentally moving stiffened legs.

"Then I'll have to do something to take your mind off your aches."

She was gathered close and her lips claimed before she could protest. Not that she was able to move with the explosion within her.

"That's for the aching muscles," he said huskily. "And that's for the work above and beyond the call of duty." he added after another searing kiss.

She managed to escape and walk shakily across the room. "It works!" she said with a grin to hide how hard she clung to the door. "But don't think that's the answer to getting me to take on more jobs!"

He threw back his head with a roar of laughter. "Then I'll have to become more persuasive," he threatened.

She hurried to the kitchen, the memory of blazing yellow eyes burning into her. How did it happen? Why should one man's arms around her create such a cataclysmic reaction?

She was acutely conscious of his eyes following her every move as she served aromatic bowls of thick soup for everyone's lunch. Every time she glanced his way, she met his warm, speculative look.

It was a man's examination, and the woman in her responded. She knew she glowed, still under the effects of his lovemaking. *Careful, girl,* she cautioned herself, but she was too bemused by the memory of his exploring kisses and the sensation of his muscular body hard against hers.

"Coming to finish the folders?" Wyatt challenged as they leaned back in their chairs, replete from the hearty soup.

"What folders?" Dave asked.

Wyatt indicated his desk. "Jennie has been at work again."

Fred whistled in admiration. "The impossible has been accomplished! We can't let you escape now if you've worked your way through that mess. Now you have to stay to keep it that way!"

Jennie shook her head. "I have only another week. Once the family is back on its feet and Grace can take over, I'll have outlived my usefulness. I do have to get back to my typewriter and make a living."

Wyatt's face was expressionless. "Then I insist you finish the folders now before you leave."

She winced as she rose to replenish the coffee and a gleam flickered in his eyes.

"Sore muscles?" he murmured. "Perhaps you need another treatment."

Fred had been thoughtfully watching the two of them. His eyes crinkled as he looked at his brother.

"Have you found a new treatment?" he asked. "Would it do for the horses?"

"Not *that* new," said Wyatt, "and none that you have not tried for yourself."

Jennie choked on her coffee. "I'd better

clear the table," she muttered and fled to the kitchen.

Again Wyatt departed after dinner.

"Lorraine?" Ruth asked as they heard his car move down the drive.

Dave shrugged, "I guess. He never tells us whom he goes out with, but since she's back in circulation I daresay he's wasting no time."

"You've seen her, Fred. What does she look like after ten years?" Ruth persisted.

He pursed his lips in thought. "Like she always did, only more so," he finally admitted. "Ten pounds heavier, but all in the right places. More daring about her clothes."

Dave looked up with interest. "Well! I see I missed something!"

"Down boy!" Ruth laughed. "The poor Franjules. They are so conventional. Even in school Lorraine used to try to shock us."

"They never could control her," Fred agreed. "They must have breathed a sigh of relief when she was married."

"Yes, even though they were obviously disappointed it wasn't Wyatt," Ruth added.

"Well, Big Brother has the chance at another try," Dave said. "She obviously isn't hard to take, and the Franjules would be forever thankful to have her settled nearby, and happy to have him inherit their holdings."

"I don't know if that is what he wants,"

Fred said, his gaze darted an instant to Jennie's bent head.

"From what I've heard, she hasn't changed much," Ruth said gloomily. "What Lorraine wants, Lorraine always gets."

She certainly does, Jennie concurred sourly when she heard his car return after midnight. If she's what he wants, he deserves her. No doubt he would have stayed with her even later if the loading hadn't been scheduled for early in the morning. The thought haunted her until the early morning hours.

Chapter Nine

The wind was holding its breath in the first silent flush of dawn. Jennie contemplated turning over to try to regain lost sleep.

She finally threw the covers back, groggy after a night spent tossing in bed. She might resent doing this for Wyatt, the alley cat, but it was no reason the others should be denied the little comfort her hot drinks gave.

It was bitterly cold and Caroline's little car growled reluctantly to life. The gravelly lane crackled underfoot like breaking ice, though the only moisture was the thick clouds forming with every breath.

The heater took a while to combat the chill in the car, and by the time she reached the loading area, she was shivering with the cold.

Heavens, how did the men manage to work in such frigid conditions! Even the shaggy dogs had little to do as the sheep moved stiffly up the ramps, too cold to offer resistance.

The truckers, wise to the weather, wore ski

masks. Even so, their faces were red when the masks were rolled up so they could drink.

"I heard about this treat," one said, smacking his lips upon tasting the brandy in the coffee. "The word is out you make the best coffee around. You won't have trouble getting truckers here from now on!"

"This soup isn't bad either," the other one put in. "This isn't just melted boullion cubes like we've had at some places."

She felt yellow eyes on her, but she avoided meeting them. Would his beloved Lorraine do this after they were married? She couldn't imagine her willingly getting out of a warm bed to extend herself.

The brothers had put in an order for flapjacks, and she had a huge mound ready when they finally returned. It was devoured hungrily, and she marveled at the hard work these men did without protest.

They worked together amazingly well and she felt a flash of guilt for stirring dissension among them. *Cherchez la femme.* It wouldn't be hard for Wyatt to discover who was rocking his orderly life if the women kept pressuring for their own homes.

"That's the last of the flock for market," Wyatt said with satisfaction as he pushed aside his plate. "The price has held for a change and we should be sitting well if we don't have too hard a winter."

The three brothers knocked the wooden table solemnly at his announcement. The superstitious gesture indicated their precarious dependency upon weather.

Wyatt gathered several boxes from a cabinet and heated powdered milk while adding measurements from the containers.

"Want me to feed them?" Fred offered.

"No, I'll do it. I thought Jennie might like to come and help."

She looked up with interest. "What am I feeding?"

"We found two droppings," Fred explained. "It happens periodically, no matter how careful we are. We plan for lambing in the spring but every once in a while a ram gets loose and we have this problem. Luckily it doesn't happen often. There is no way we can find the mothers once they are loaded. We have old Nellie who takes them on, but she's too old to have much milk.

"She's an old dam who thinks her only purpose in life is to care for orphan lambs. She's a darn nuisance at times because she also tries to take them away from their mothers. But in cases like this, or where their mothers reject them, she earns her keep. She keeps them clean and warm, and in this weather, that's something."

Jennie's face clouded with consternation. "Oh, but those poor mothers to be parted from their young."

A large hand came heavily on her shoulder. "Whoa, city gal," Wyatt said sternly. "This is no children's zoo with pets. This is a ranch, where sheep are a commodity. You need to keep your thinking straight if you're to live on a ranch."

She pulled away from his touch, resentful over his cold logical approach to something her warm heart rebelled against.

"Then it's lucky I won't have to live on one, isn't it!" she snapped. "I still think it's cruel to separate a mother from her baby."

He filled two quart soda bottles with the warm mixture. "Then you won't be interested in helping feeding them," he said.

"I didn't say that," she said with irritation. "Of course I'd love to help."

Old Nellie eyed them beligerently when they approached the stall. She had finished cleaning the lambs, turning them into silken fluff balls. They were soon working hungrily on the improvised bottles.

"They're adorable even if their table manners are atrocious," Jennie cried, her face alight with delight. "How can they turn into such fat plodding animals when they grow up!"

"You'd plod too if you carried their wool load. Wait until you see them in spring after shearing. They become half their size."

"You'll have to invite me back," she said,

smiling over the sated lambs wobbling back to their foster mother on still unsteady legs.

"You have an open invitation to come whenever you can. In fact, the invitation still stands to take up regular quarters here. There will be plenty of room when we move the furniture from the bedroom."

A nerve quivered through her. "Persistent, aren't you?" she chided. "But you're not fooling me. You're luring me for my cooking. What happens when you marry? I'll be out on my ear."

"I don't know about that," he grinned. "If my wife wants me, she'll have to take my cook also."

She glanced at him balefully.

"Until I snare a wife, you're safe," he said, unperturbed. "What do you say; will you take me up on my offer?"

What if she confounded him and took him seriously? The thought ran a quiver through her. That chemistry exploded between them too easily.

"I doubt it," she answered. "You have three women here already. A fourth is unnecessary."

"You mean you would demand full control of a house if you lived in one?"

She wished she could read his mind behind those hooded eyes.

"We seem to be talking at cross-purposes.

As a cook, I have no rights. But if I were married, yes, I would want to be the lone woman in charge of not only the kitchen but my house. Selfish perhaps, but I wouldn't want to share my husband every evening with someone else." *Now was the time to put in a plug for Ruth.* "I fully endorse Ruth and Dave's desire for their own place. No woman is happy until she has her own nest."

His face became shuttered and she knew she had intruded into a delicate area. The teasing was over and she drew the jacket close in preparation to brave the waiting cold winds.

"Do you have work to do?" she asked. "If you tell me the formula and when they have to be fed, I'll pinch-hit as a foster mother."

"It won't be necessary," he said coolly.

The rejection came as a slap after the warmth they had shared while feeding the lambs. *Impossible man! Was his family so sacrosanct to him she couldn't give an opinion?*

Burying her chin in the thick wool collar, she dashed to the house. Being in contact with that difficult man was too abrasive. Every time she thought their relationship was on a balanced keel, he tipped the boat, throwing her into icy waters.

Tomorrow Caroline would be back and Jennie would have to accompany him to his Lorraine's party. She rebelled at the thought but reasoned it was small enough return for the good times they had shared. Then, before her cousin compounded Wyatt's animosity by announcing they, too, desired to escape his control, she'd be gone.

A despondency settled on her while she busied herself in the kitchen, preparing extras for several days. She'd want free time to be with her cousin these last days.

But the thought kept surfacing. *Wyatt and Lorraine.* How deep was his involvement? Was the past forgiven, leaving a clear path for further commitment? She gnawed tentatively at the edge of the questions, but would not bite deeply. She refused to examine why she should care about two people who shortly would be out of her life. Once Caroline had her own place, there would be no reason to return to this ranch. . . .

"This is a mean and nasty thing you're doing," Fred said, appearing at the door. "I'm supposed to be hard at work over a new design, but that delicious aroma has crept into my room. How about a snack for me?"

"I'm in line also," Wyatt said, coming in behind his brother.

Ruth and Dave joined them. Jennie watched with amusement how the simple sugar cookies disappeared.

"They were for an occasional *snack,*" she said dryly. "Not for a whole meal. We're low on flour and I can't make any more."

"I'll double the amount of the next order," Wyatt answered complacently.

Fred refilled the coffee cups as they sat comfortably around the kitchen table. "I called the Hasting Ranch. Bob is expected before lunch tomorrow, and Cary is flying in with him. It will be good to have her back," he added almost to himself.

The admission came softly, and Jennie smiled in understanding. Did Caroline fully appreciate what a wonderful husband she had? So many woman slid into complacency. If she ever found a man to love, she'd follow that old ballad—love him in the morning, love him at night—

"Have you been to old Tom's place recently?" Wyatt asked Dave while creaming his coffee.

"No, not since the burn-off. Was it successful? That was good pastureland before he let it go."

"Yes, it seems to have done the job. We should be able to run sheep there after the spring rains. But I was thinking of the old homestead. It was a comfortable place when his wife was alive."

"I remember it as always being refreshingly cool in the summer," Ruth said. "The walls were so thick they kept out the heat. Too bad there's no one in it now. It had a great fireplace."

154

"Why don't you two run up and give it a once-over when Ruth's better? See what you think of it. If it's too small, you can always add rooms."

Ruth's eyes grew round with surprise as she realized what he was intimating.

Dave swallowed hard. "I think Ruth will have an instant cure," he said huskily. "As I recall it had an incredible view, sitting on the side of the mountain. Are you offering it to us?"

"If it meets your needs. As Ruth said it has a lot of good features and standing idle is the worst thing for a house."

"Besides, I have an underhanded reason behind it. I want to put a greater concentration of sheep there but would hate to leave them unguarded. That damn rustling is becoming more organized all the time. I swear we lost some from the southwest tract."

Ruth jumped up from the table to hug her brother-in-law. "And here we were worried how we'd manage building a large enough house and you had the solution all the time!"

"What are you going to do with this big house?" Dave asked, concern wrinkling his brow.

"I'll turn your wing into an office suite. I'm crowded in the library. I hated turning it into a workroom. Besides, now that I have married off my brothers, I might think of taking a wife also. That should eventually take care of the bedrooms." A small smile lifted his lips as he stared down at his cup.

Lorraine! Jennie turned cold, and she curled her hands around the coffee mug, seeking its warmth.

"Well!" Fred said heartily. "Don't keep us in suspense. Who's the lucky woman?"

"You'll be the first to know once she accepts me," he answered smoothly.

It was the perfect exit line and he took advantage of it to leave for the living room.

"What! Honoring us with your presence tonight?" Fred asked Wyatt when they had settled in the living room after dinner. "Or are you off to greener pastures?"

Ignoring their teasing, Wyatt threw another log on the fire.

"He's giving the poor girl a break," Dave said, adding slyly, "she needs all the beauty sleep she can get for the big night tomorrow."

Jennie was gripped by a way of nausea. *I must be getting the flu after all,* she thought.

"Something wrong, Jennie?" Fred asked. "You look pale."

"Just a little tired," she said slowly. "I think I'll bid for an early bed and say good-night."

Wyatt was by her side instantly, ushering her to the stairs. "You do look pale," he said with concern. "You're always at the far side of the room and I couldn't see. You're not catching the bug, are you?"

156

"I'm not sure. A good night's sleep should take care of things."

"Soak in a hot tub then take two aspirins," he prescribed. "Call when you're ready for bed and I'll bring up a hot toddy."

"I'll survive. No need to be concerned."

"Concerned! of course I am! You've been spoiling us, and now it's time for us to do some in return. Upstairs. Fast." he ordered.

"Before you drink it, you better be in bed," Fred called after her. "From experience, we warn you, his drink will lay you flat."

Jennie hurried to comply, embarrassed over the attention.

"How can you stay warm wearing that thing!" It was Wyatt, standing with a steaming mug by Jennie's bedroom door.

"It's all that's necessary in a steam-heated apartment," she said, determinedly ignoring the look in his eyes as he took in her slim figure outlined by the blue wisp of nylon. He could at least have waited for her to answer his knock!

Well, if he showed no embarrassment, she was darned if she would. She slid under covers and held out her hand for the mug.

The mattress sagged as he sat on the edge of her bed.

"Drink slowly. It's hot. I put in honey and laced it with rum."

"The fumes are enough to put me to sleep," she protested, taking a cautious sip.

A finger moved a long strand of silky hair from her cheek. "That is the object," he said softly. "I can't have you sick. We're showing you off tomorrow, remember. A red nose might not match your dress."

She eyed him warily over the brim of the mug. He didn't act like a man about to be engaged to someone else.

But then, how did she expect him to act? She had learned how he controlled his emotions.

"I think it was wonderful of you to offer that house to Ruth and Dave," she said. "From what she was telling me it has lots of possibilities."

"I hope it meets with your approval."

"My approval?" she asked in surprise. "What have I to do with it?"

The corners of his mouth quirked. "You said you wouldn't take on the job as permanent cook if there were too many women around. I have just eliminated one."

She wrinkled her nose at him. "I see you're making it hard for me to resist," she said, handing him the empty mug before snuggling under the covers.

He tucked the blanket over her shoulder and leaned over to place a chaste kiss on her lips. "That's the whole idea," he whispered with a satisfied chuckle. He dimmed the light as he walked out.

Fred had been right, his toddy was lethal. Her eyes closed even as she tried to decipher his words. Did he mean . . . was she imagining . . . had she heard . . . she could no longer fight off sleep.

Chapter Ten

Jennie yawned and stretched. The hot toddy had accomplished two things. It insured a much-needed restful sleep and banished the last of her aching muscles.

She stretched again, and stopped short at the knock on her open door. Wyatt stood there, a tray in his hands. She sat up in surprise. A breakfast tray brought by *Wyatt*?

"How nice!" she exclaimed, sitting up hastily to smooth the blanket for placement. "I'm not sick, though the thought is lovely. You must patent that mixture, Wyatt. It put me to sleep like a baby."

"I'm going to have to do something about you before you get pneumonia," he said with a sigh.

She followed his gaze and fought desperately against the flush rising to her cheeks. The low-cut lacy décolleté of her gown seductively accented the soft curve of her breasts. Drat those man-eyes gleaming with appreciation!"

"If you hand me the sweater on the chair," she said, "I'll be presentable. I'll have to buy a flannel nightgown if you keep coming in here."

"Perhaps it would be better," he grinned, removing a second mug of coffee from the tray and settling in a chair. "It would be easier on my blood pressure."

She swallowed a biting retort along with the orange juice. No need to act adolescent over the incident. If ignored, it would recede to its proper insignificance.

"I apologize for not being up early. Who made breakfast?" she asked.

"You forget we were bachelors for a number of years. We all manage a passable skillet."

"With the twins so much better, I thought Grace was back to kitchen duty."

His lips firmed. "She's taking care of them for another week until Ruth can take over."

"Has Fred left to get Caroline?"

His eyes narrowed as he watched her. "He was going to ask you to go with him but I told him not to wake you up."

"It aill be good to see her," she said brightly, uncomfortable under his unwavering gaze. "I came on her express wish, yet have seen very little of her. Next time we'll have to plan better." She was babbling foolishly, she knew, but she couldn't stop.

"Yes, I was surprised she took off like that. What's the story behind it all?"

Jennie blinked. So he *was* suspicious.

"I'm not following you," she said, but her face gave her away.

He studied her for a moment, then gave a wry smile. "Never mind," he said. "It will surface in due time."

Caroline arrived after lunch, her glowing face broadcasting the success of her trip. She brought with her the pent up energy and the swift movements of the city, and Jennie realized how she herself had succumbed to the slow, even pace of ranch life.

Caroline was too wound up, too aggressive in her movements. The realization shocked Jennie. This was the way her cousin had been in Chicago, a ball of fire. She had forgotten that aspect of her, had only been conscious of her restlessness.

The city life was her lifeblood, and the transfusion had her moving with the swift decisive walk of a woman electrically alive, brimming with ideas.

Fred, in contrast, had a wary look. They must have had a long talk on the ride back, yet from the occasional frowning glances Caroline gave her husband, Jennie knew no positive commitment had been made.

"You don't have to tell me the outcome of your trip," Jennie said when they were finally alone. "It's written all over you."

"Oh, Jennie!" she enthused. "I've never felt

so alive, so completely in my element. How did I ever think I could hibernate on a ranch! I live and breathe over the challenges from the business world. They were bowled over by Fred's designs. Every store buyer promised to take whatever he could turn out at fantastic prices. He just has to move to the city where I don't have to depend on this crazy way of traveling."

"You don't have to make those trips every day," Jennie said gently. "You can meet Fred's wishes halfway."

A frown creased her smooth forehead. "That's what he said, but I pointed out he would need larger quarters to turn out the jewelry already on order. He always said he needed more sophisticated machinery to do a better job. He should hire someone to do the basic work for him so he can concentrate on the finished product."

Her quick mind was already envisioning expansion. Would her enthusiasm carry Fred along in its fast current?

And what of Wyatt? Would he let yet another brother take off? Dave at least was still part of the ranch. Fred would be lost forever once he stepped away from the east wing.

Still, Fred was wavering. If Wyatt exerted pressure, saying he needed him, would his deep sense of obligation negate his wife's insistent clamor to return to city life?

Feeling the uncertainty hovering in the air, Jennie decided to change the subject.

"Did Fred have time to tell you we are invited to a party tonight at the Franjule ranch?" she asked. "I'll have to borrow something from you. I didn't bring anything fancy enough for it."

Immediately, Caroline went to her clothes closet to fling open the door. Caroline as a clothes buyer had enjoyed the pick of high style fashions.

Needless to say, I have seldom worn these," she said with a trace of bitterness. "They're a year old, but we should be able to come up with something to uphold the Dubrow honor."

They settled on a golden chiffon for Jennie, a dress she had loved on first sight. Caroline chose a flaming red creation with a pencil slim skirt slit up on leg.

The tryout over, they removed the dresses. Out of nowhere, Caroline casually dropped the news.

"My foolish brother-in-law is getting engaged."

"Engaged?" The word came out in a whisper. *Then it was definite.* "How do you know?"

"He found this gorgeous garnet and had Fred cut and polish it. He designed a terrific ring, bracketing it in diamonds. He wanted it for tonight. It's spectacular. I wouldn't mind having it myself."

A shock wave went through Jennie. Wyatt was using her garnet!

"Oh, dear, I shouldn't be telling you, but I'm ready to explode over the fool. He swore Fred to secrecy but I happened to overhear it."

Jennie licked dry lips. "That doesn't mean he's getting engaged."

Caroline gave an unladylike hoot. "Can you imagine a man like our Wyatt having a ring made for any other reason? With Lorraine back, I'm afraid it's a foregone conclusion."

Jennie sat there woodenly, too numb to move. It figured, of course. If he were giving Dave and Ruth old Tom's homestead, what better way to recoup losses than to marry into the rich Franjule land? Especially since it was spiced by a ripe, giving daughter who made it only too plain what she wanted! Lorraine had escaped him once. He would not let it happen again.

Jennie drew a deep breath to relieve the sharp ache in her chest. With startling clarity she knew why she was reacting this way. She could evade it no longer. She was in love with Wyatt Dubrow. What a fool she had been to let this broad-shouldered, arrogant man stroll into her heart!

"When do we congratulate them?" she whispered.

Caroline stopped her pacing to look questioningly at her cousin. Her eyes widened in surprise upon seeing the blanched face, the hands clenched on her lap.

"Oh, Jennie, love, I didn't know!" she cried, hurrying over to kneel by her. "Has that big oaf been making passes at you?"

"Passes?" Jennie raised a stricken face. "That's a laugh! You heard how he likes to flay me."

With vicious sweeps she eradicated each memory of the special times, the gentle, happy times, the shared humor and laughter. The only way she could survive was to recapture the anger from past caustic words.

"I know, I know," Caroline said, frowning. "We couldn't figure out what hit him. I was hoping it would smooth out while I was away. In fact, when I saw how he was watching you this afternoon . . ."

Jennie shivered. "He's watching me all right. Like a hawk. I dream about those yellow eyes following me. You know why, don't you?" she confessed bitterly, desperately fanning her anger.

"He thinks I'm a home wrecker. Me, plain Jennifer Robbins. What a laugh! Whenever I talk to Dave or Fred, he's ready to pounce!"

Caroline looked at her with amazement. Slowly the look of concern faded and her mouth twitched.

"Hm. Yes. I didn't realize it, but that could be the reason." She lit a cigarette while eyeing the distraught girl. "Big Brother runs to basic emotions after all," she mused complacently. "Look, love, this engagement thing is all conjecture. You take a nice hot tub, then I'll come to do your hair. Thank goodness with my short cut, I don't have to fuss."

"I'm not going," Jennie said obstinately.

"You most certainly are," Caroline shot back. "Since when does a Robbins give any man the satisfaction he can twist her into knots?"

The cousins stared at each other until Jennie lowered her lashes. There was a curious relief knowing her new found knowledge was shared with Caroline, the way they had shared before. She didn't have to carry this heartache alone. . . .

"Will there be dancing?" Caroline asked as they stepped into the town car to go to the party.

"Yes," Wyatt replied. "They've scrubbed out the tractor barn and have been painting and decorating all week. They've also put in heat."

Fred whistled. "It must be costing Basil a bundle!"

"Anything Lorraine wants, Lorraine gets," Caroline put in dryly.

It was a constant refrain, one Jennie heard whenever Lorraine was mentioned. And now she realized with a pang that it was all too true.

There were already several cars parked by the colorfully spotlighted barn and they hurried in to escape the cold wind.

Mrs. Franjule was short and square, a heavy bosomed woman, still retaining some of the good looks her daughter had inherited. She greeted Wyatt as if he were already a son, while Mr. Franjule put his arm across Wyatt's shoulders in an attempt to draw him next to him in the receiving line.

Wyatt managed to extricate himself to introduce Jennie. Their smiles were friendly, but perfunctory. They were only interested in the man next to her.

Lorraine was spectacular in an electric blue gown shot with gold. A scarf sedately covered her shoulders, and Jennie wondered if it was worn to appease her parents.

"Wyatt!" she cried. Her hands went to his shoulders, pulling him down to meet her full, moist lips. "I've been waiting for you. As soon as a few more people arrive, I can get away from this silly reception line mother dotes on. This is our evening!"

Jennie turned away, not wanting to hear further. It was as everyone suspected. *What Lorraine wants, Lorraine gets.*

Caroline lead Jennie to a group of friends. Surprisingly, Wyatt came also. She wanted to tell him not to feel obligated to escort her further, but the opportunity didn't arise as she was busily introduced to a constant change of faces.

Then the music started, and she was on the dance floor, held in his arms. She had always loved dancing, but now was wound tight as a spring. Was this his duty dance for the evening?

"Relax, city girl," he murmured into her hair. "The band isn't the greatest, but they try hard."

Suddenly she didn't care about any announcement to be made later, or the resulting heartache. She was in the arms of the man she loved and she'd take every drop of pleasure she could out of it.

The music was a slow foxtrot for the old-timers and she snuggled against him. His arm tightened, pulling her closer. She moved as in a dream, content there was no attempt at conversation to intrude on her bliss.

It had to end of course, and she swallowed a little moan of regret when he removed his arms.

Lorraine materialized by them, towing along a tall, rawboned man with sunbleached hair.

"Willy has been dying to meet your house guest, darling," she said silkily. "Come, this dance is ours!" She drew Wyatt away.

Willy stared after them, then gave a faint shrug. "She hasn't changed. She's still chasing him. Maybe her technique has improved with time. But she's right, I did want to meet the loveliest girl here. Shall we dance?"

Jennie recalled the conversation in the car. This was Willy who had a crush on Lorraine, yet he wasn't letting himself be decimated by her behavior. She could learn a lesson from him.

"You are the belle of the ball, Jennie," Fred said, dodging a couple on the dance floor to cut in on Willy. "Everyone is asking about you except a certain hostess. Do you have the feeling daggers are being sent your way?"

The smile became stiff. "She has nothing to worry about. She has Wyatt wrapped around her finger where she wants him."

He examined the flushed face, seeing her tight expression, and gave a sigh. "He hasn't had much choice. She's kept a hammerlock hold on him and he's too much of a gentleman to make a scene. The Franjules are good friends of ours."

"You don't have to make excuses for him," she said, a smile painted brightly on her face. "He brought me, but he was only being polite to the house guest until he was with her."

He shook his head as he drew her closer. She closed her eyes as she rested her cheek on his shoulder. She had a suspicion Fred knew what was happening to her. Dear Fred. He was a gentle teddy bear of a man, a kind cousin-in-law, acting the protective big brother.

"Cary tell you about the success of her trip?" he asked.

"Yes, I'm so thrilled for you both. She needs something like that to stimulate her. I'm afraid she was getting restless so far from the activities she has always thrived upon."

"I know," he said somberly, leading from the floor as the dance ended. "I knew I was taking a calculated risk in bringing her to the ranch, hoping she would adjust. She tried. I know she did, but it isn't for her.

"I told her during the last dance I was going to tell Wyatt tonight when we get home that we would be leaving as soon as he made arrangements for a replacement. Hell, he can hire several men to help for what he gives me!" he said grimly.

Her hand offered comfort as she placed it on his arm. The muscles were tense, and she knew as well as he that it wasn't the money or the manpower that would bother his brother.

Jennie reached up to place a consoling kiss on his cheek. As she did so, she was suddenly conscious of blazing yellow eyes flicking contemptuously over her before they turned scornfully away.

Not again! she cried silently. Wyatt had seen the kiss and was misinterpreting it once more.

Lorraine was by his side, her arm tight around his, much as Fred had described. Her look was triumphant as she slowly untied the scarf and dropped its camouflage.

Dimly Jennie heard someone give a wolf whistle. She had been correct. The scarf had been worn to appease her conservative parents. Her décolleté left nothing to the imagination. *How is that affecting your blood pressure, Mr. Dubrow?* Jennie thought bitterly. Her lacy nightgown had been virginal in comparison. She moved away, not wanting to see the expression on his face. Suddenly it was hot in the room, and only the knowledge of the bitter wind outside prevented her from escaping into the welcoming darkness. Surely there must be a cooler spot where she could reassemble her scattered wits.

A group of potted plants in a corner caught her eye. She could hide behind them until she could force the smile back on her face. Would the evening never end?

She made her way to the greenery to find a doorway was hidden behind the foliage, a dim light glowing from its depth. Just what she wanted.

She paused in the opening, letting her eyes adjust to the gloom. It was a small lean-to and had been decorated into a little retreat. There were additional potted plants and wide reclining porch settees. As she approached she heard a low seductive laugh that set her nerves tingling. Lorraine! And the tall figure bending over her could only be Wyatt! Jennie started to back away, suppressing a moan of pain.

But Wyatt had sensed her presence. Before she could turn away and flee, he had seen her. For an instant, his mocking eyes met hers. Then, slowly and insolently he bent his head to meet Lorraine's waiting lips.

Jennie was hardly conscious of how she got back to the other room.

Caroline spotted her by the door. She broke away from Fred and came over to her. "What in the world is the matter, Jen?" she asked. "You look as white as a ghost!"

Jennie's lips quivered. "Is there some way I can get a ride home? I have a terrible headache." She knew her excuse sounded unconvincing, but she was past caring.

"There's no such thing as a taxi service here," Caroline said. Her eyes travelled thoughtfully over her cousin's face. "But, don't worry, I'll tell Fred and we'll leave right away. It's been a long day for me, also."

"But Wyatt won't want to leave," Jennie said dully.

"Do you know where he is?" Basil Franjule hurried over to them, his face creased with anxiety. "Wyatt. I need him."

Should she tell Basil where he could find Wyatt?

"I'm here, what do you want?" Wyatt appeared next to them, his face hard.

"The phone call came," the short man said

excitedly. "It's the one we've been waiting for. They've been located on the Corrdry ranch. It would happen the night we have a party, but perhaps that is why they planned it."

"Damn!" Wyatt exploded, looking down at his clothes. "Well, we can't help our outfits. I'll get Fred and you round up the others."

"That ends the party," Caroline said in a tight voice. Jennie looked at her with bewilderment.

"Rustlers," she explained tersely. "The stakeouts have finally paid off. It must be the big operation they were expecting. I only hope no one gets trigger-happy."

The same worry was reflected on each wife's face as husbands were kissed good-bye. The men, dressed handsomely in formal clothes, looked incongruous with faces now hard with resolution.

"Drive carefully," Fred said, his hand on Caroline's cheek. "We're going in one of Basil's trucks."

Wyatt's mouth thinned into a grim line. Slowly, as if against his will, a finger came up to lift one of the curls caressing Jennie's cheek. Then he was gone.

Shaken by his gesture, Jennie remained motionless. *Don't torture me like that!* her heart cried.

Everyone said good-night to the hostess. It was not a pleasant way for a party to end, but this emergency came first. If they didn't succeed in capturing the rustlers, the losses would be heavy.

The party had broken up to soon. There had not even been time to announce the engagement.

Chapter Eleven

The first pale streaks were in the sky when the men finally returned home.

Jennie, who had slept fitfully, was up when she heard the heavy motor of the truck grind to a halt to drop them off.

The men slumped exhaustedly in chairs as she hurriedly made coffee and scrambled eggs for breakfast.

"Were you successful?" she asked.

"Yes," Fred answered. "We caught them in the act. It was the operation we were hoping to get."

"Then you can relax now," she said in relief.

Wyatt gave a bitter shrug. "There was a lot spent on their rigs. Someone with an awful lot of money was behind them, and they'll find others to man another setup. As long as the price of meat stays high, it is worth their while to come in at night and butcher a flock."

The men exchanged glances. No mention was made of the exchange of gunfire. A truck driver had been critically wounded, and a bullet had grazed the head of another . It had been a close thing.

The sheriff had quickly deputized all and thanked them when it was all over. Perhaps they'd get some information from them before the lawyers came with bail. Perhaps, but not likely. They were too well organized.

It was a bitter pill to swallow. The only recourse the ranchers had was to continue the watches.

The men took quick showers to get rid of the grime. Jennie listened to Wyatt move around in his room. As always, when she knew he was safely home, she, too, was able to go back to sleep.

The men went out after lunch to catch up on their jobs. Caroline joined her in the kitchen, helping with peeling the vegetables.

"Fred told me he was going to tell Wyatt about your plans last night," Jennie said. "Too bad the rustlers took priority."

Caroline looked up, her face aglow. "But he did. On the ride to the Corrdry ranch, he told him all about it."

"What did he say?"

"Fred was amazed over how well he took it. In fact, he even looked pleased and agreed it wouldn't be a bad idea. He said the rooms were always there if the venture didn't prove a success."

She gave a little laugh. "It's funny now

when you think about it. Both brothers felt so obligated to stay, and all they had to do was tell him they wanted a change. Fred couldn't get over it. Wyatt almost seemed relieved to have us go. It was as if he had other plans now."

"Lorraine," Jennie muttered. "Both you and Ruth said she would want to be queen without another woman's interference."

"Mm, I guess so. But I still can't see her filling those other bedrooms as Wyatt hinted. Children aren't part of her plan in life and I can't imagine him being so blind as not to realize that."

After dinner the family gathered together again in the living room.

Jennie had lived through a lifetime of emotional conflicts, and was nerve-shatteringly afraid of another confrontation. The memory of icy yellow eyes condemning her last night was mixed with the hot defiance later in that dim room.

He had reduced her to a bundle of nerves, jumping when he was near her, avoiding meeting his gaze she found too often on her. He didn't have to stand watch anymore. He could concentrate on Lorraine.

She would be happy when the evening was over. Her torment was making her feverish. She would have to tell Caroline she was leaving. Wyatt still hadn't given the ring to Lorraine, and she only hoped she was far away when it happened.

Fred and Caroline were discussing a trip in the morning to Bailey's *Arroyo* for a last look for stones before they started house hunting. They weren't certain where would be the best place to settle, but Jennie could see their excitement over the quest.

Lucky people! To have the whole world before them. To explore it together. What a lovely word that was—together.

She was very much in the way now. Her cousin had more pressing things to occupy herself with and Grace was only too eager to take over the kitchen again.

"Want to come with us?" Caroline asked.

Jennie caught her breath. It would be too painful to revisit that valley, to see where they had been entwined in so breathless a passionate embrace during the dust storm, its fury matching their runaway emotions.

"We'll see about that in the morning," she said, forcing a smile, "but I have a feeling that I ought to be thinking about leaving, it's been over two weeks, you know—" She rose swiftly, before anyone could remonstrate. She was vaguely aware of Fred making a move toward her before Caroline placed a restraining hand on his arm. There was no word from Wyatt. He was evidently thankful that she was thinking of leaving. She could only be an embarrassment now that Lorraine was claiming his time.

The pain grew, clawing at her chest as she ran up the stairs. She knew in time it would diminish to a dull ache she could live with, but right now it made it difficult to breathe. She allowed the tears to flow when she had reached the safety of her room. The fact that Wyatt had said nothing about her staying longer proved how little he thought of her. How gullible she had been to ever imagine that those few precious times in his arms meant anything to him! Now she realized that it had all been wishful thinking, a grasping at a fool's paradise.

She should have remembered that first night and his kiss which branded her with contempt. Later he had found what an easy conquest she was. Now she wondered why he had stopped short of taking what he so evidently wanted and knew she was willing to give. She collapsed on the bed, burying her hot face in the cool linen in an agony of despair.

When there were no tears left, she dragged out her suitcases. One thing was certain, she could never face any of them again. She'd leave at the crack of dawn. His Lordship would no doubt breathe a sigh of relief upon finding she'd left. Her disrupting influence would be gone.

As for Caroline—she was wrapped in excited anticipation of the new life opening for her. A phone call later would provide explanation enough. Her cousin knew of her true emotional involvement and would understand, smooth any awkwardness.

By the time the suitcases were packed, she was exhausted. She crept into bed, certain the turmoil tearing through her would prevent sleep from reaching her. But soon her eyes closed and her drawn face relaxed in a deep sleep.

Chapter Twelve

Jennie felt lips brush softly against hers. The kiss deepened and demanded. A hand moved lightly along the curve of her neck, pushing at the lace of her nightgown to move caressingly, knowingly, over her breasts until she could feel them swell in quick response. His mouth trailed a line of fire along its path, and she melted against the man whom her heart, her soul, her body, craved.

She awoke with a start. A bright ray of sunshine streamed in on her pillow. She blinked in its glare. Slowly, the thunder in her heart stilled, to be succeeded by an engulfing wave of desolation as she remembered the reality. Too often she had burned her way through that dream. But now there was no hope of a happy ending. Never in her waking life would she find fullfillment with the only man she had ever loved.

She glanced at the clock and jumped out of bed. Nine o'clock! Her careful plan to escape at dawn was a thing of the past.

Still, with luck, she could go unnoticed. Caroline and Fred would have left early to reach Bailey's little valley to search for the streaked stones he wanted.

She knew the routine by now.

The men, as usual, would be off taking care of the innumerable jobs on the ranch. Ruth would be resting while Grace took care of the twins.

She opened the door and listened at the head of the stairs. All was quiet. Someone else had made breakfast. They would never miss her, she thought bitterly.

A shower first, she decided, grabbing her bathrobe. She'd leave in style even if there was no one to bid her good-bye.

Her lips quivered in self-pity and she shut the bathroom door with an unnecessary slam. She did not hear the door of the truck downstairs slam at the same time.

The hot shower did its job of untying tense muscles and soothing screaming nerves. She rubbed herself dry, blanking her mind to all thoughts, willing her body to remain in this relaxed stupor. She would loose this calm control soon enough.

She ran quietly down the hall even though no on was about, and closed her door carefully behind her. Her mind was on the suit she had left unpacked. Would it be warm enough for the mountains? It was cold going over the twisting roads.

"Going somewhere?"

Jennie let out a sharp gasp as she clutched her loose bathrobe.

Wyatt was leaning against the closet door, his arms bent across his chest while a foot rested on a suitcase.

He was the hawk again, his face set in grim lines, drawing the bony planes in sharp relief. The yellow eyes were watchful, giving every indication he was ready to pounce.

"What are you doing here?" she asked nervously.

"I live here."

She shook her head in a daze. Now how was she going to escape!

"I—I thought you were out on the ranch."

"Evidently."

She took a deep breath, hoping desperately to reorganize her scattered wits. "If you will please go, I'll get dressed. I want to leave."

"No."

"No?"

"No, I'm not going. No, you are not leaving."

She pulled the sash tight on her robe with nerveless fingers.

"I don't understand. Last night you seemed eager to have me go," she reminded him bitterly.

"What in heaven's name, woman, are you talking about?" His face was genuinely puzzled.

184

"You didn't seem too upset last night when I suggested leaving."

"If you remember, you neglected to mention that you were leaving today. I am hardly a mind reader, you know." His eyes were cold, yellow topaz.

"But surely, you gathered—you knew—when I ran from the room—"

"I knew no such thing," he said firmly. "Though I could see you were upset for some fool reason of your own, I didn't think it was exactly the time to say what I wanted to say in front of the whole family. It's not exactly the time or place to propose to a girl."

Jennie's mouth dropped open. "Propose?" she stammered. "And what about your precious Lorraine?"

"Lorraine?" It was his turn to look surprised.

"Yes, Lorraine, the woman you enjoyed kissing in the shed. Surely, you remember that?"

"Yes, and you kissed Fred."

Her eyes grew wide. So that was the answer!

"It was a spontaneous thing," she protested. "He had just told me he and Caroline had solved their differences. I was so happy for them I kissed him on the cheek. It didn't mean anything!"

Wyatt raised his hand and long fingers slid along the outline of her cheek.

185

"Do you know what havoc you have been causing me, woman?" he murmured. "From the first moment you stepped out of this room and almost into my arms, I've wanted you there. You have no idea how I fought it. I didn't want you coming into my life, changing it. You were from the city and I could see what was happening to Fred and Cary. But, Lord, how you changed it. I even had to fight being jealous of my brothers even while knowing it was all in my imagination."

When Wyatt finished his confession, Jennie's lips parted, as if to speak. Then she moved away, walking blindly as full understanding flooded her. She paused, stopped by the bed. In a minute she knew she would be placing her life irrevocably into this man's hands, and she wondered at the magnitude of what she was doing. But before she committed herself she needed one last answer.

"About Lorraine. Were you ever engaged?"

He moved his shoulder in an impatient gesture. "You're gnawing on an old bone, Jennie. I'll tell you the truth in case you ever hear other versions and then I never want to hear the subject again.

"I was twenty-one, fresh out of college. Girls were nothing new to me and Lorraine was one I dated. She was from around here. There were few enough young girls to date. She soon started talking wedding bells but I wasn't ready, especially when she pressed for living in the city. Then when my parents died, I had no time for other commitments. She quickly found someone else who was willing to take her away. That's the complete story. No frills, no lost love. I've heard some of the stories floating around and they are not true."

Jenny was almost giddy with relief. All that heartache for nothing!

He came closer until they almost touched.

"Jennie?" he said softly.

She smiled up at him, ready for his question. All doubts were laid to rest.

"Yes, Wyatt?"

"Do you hear what I'm saying? I love you. I need you, not only now but for the rest of my life. Will you marry me?"

"Of course," she whispered, and the glow on her face made him catch his breath.

His hand came out of his pocket and slipped a ring over her finger.

"It's the garnet you found!" she exclaimed.

He nodded. "I had Fred design it." A faint smile curved his lips. "When I found it I thought, now there's a stone which would make an attractive ring. Then when I came back and saw you asleep on the rug under the cottonwood tree, I knew it was for you."

His finger was back, moving tenderly along the warm curve of her cheek as he gazed at her in wonderment.

"I vowed one spitfire of a girl wasn't going to

187

disturb my life. But you sneaked in and soon occupied every corner of my being. Oh, Jennie, love!"

Her arms went up and around his neck. Under her fingers his hair felt strong and wiry, vital as the man.

His arms were iron bands as he swept her close. He gave a cry of triumph as he claimed her mouth.

The force of their meeting tipped them over onto the bed but it didn't stop their kiss.

Slowly, gently, his hand slid along her face, then down her neck. The robe had fallen open, offering no obstruction as tender probing fingers moved over her breasts.

Her skin flamed as his mouth followed the trail.

"Please," she whispered. "Please don't let it be a dream."

Wyatt lifted his head as he shifted his body closer. His yellow eyes were twin suns burning down at her.

"Dream? Why should it be?" he asked huskily before reclaiming her lips. "You can't get much more real than this. . . ."

Silhouette Romance

IT'S YOUR OWN SPECIAL TIME

Contemporary romances for today's women.
Each month, six very special love stories will be yours
from SILHOUETTE. Look for them wherever books are sold
or order now from the coupon below.

$1.50 each

Hampson	☐ 1 ☐ 4 ☐ 16 ☐ 27 ☐ 28 ☐ 40 ☐ 52 ☐ 64 ☐ 94	Browning	☐ 12 ☐ 38 ☐ 53 ☐ 73 ☐ 93
Stanford	☐ 6 ☐ 25 ☐ 35 ☐ 46 ☐ 58 ☐ 88	Michaels	☐ 15 ☐ 32 ☐ 61 ☐ 87
		John	☐ 17 ☐ 34 ☐ 57 ☐ 85
Hastings	☐ 13 ☐ 26 ☐ 44 ☐ 67	Beckman	☐ 8 ☐ 37 ☐ 54 ☐ 72 ☐ 96
Vitek	☐ 33 ☐ 47 ☐ 66 ☐ 84		

$1.50 each

☐ 3 Powers	☐ 29 Wildman	☐ 56 Trent	☐ 79 Halldorson
☐ 5 Goforth	☐ 30 Dixon	☐ 59 Vernon	☐ 80 Stephens
☐ 7 Lewis	☐ 31 Halldorson	☐ 60 Hill	☐ 81 Roberts
☐ 9 Wilson	☐ 36 McKay	☐ 62 Hallston	☐ 82 Dailey
☐ 10 Caine	☐ 39 Sinclair	☐ 63 Brent	☐ 83 Hallston
☐ 11 Vernon	☐ 41 Owen	☐ 69 St. George	☐ 86 Adams
☐ 14 Oliver	☐ 42 Powers	☐ 70 Afton Bonds	☐ 89 James
☐ 19 Thornton	☐ 43 Robb	☐ 71 Ripy	☐ 90 Major
☐ 20 Fulford	☐ 45 Carroll	☐ 74 Trent	☐ 92 McKay
☐ 21 Richards	☐ 48 Wildman	☐ 75 Carroll	☐ 95 Wisdom
☐ 22 Stephens	☐ 49 Wisdom	☐ 76 Hardy	☐ 97 Clay
☐ 23 Edwards	☐ 50 Scott	☐ 77 Cork	☐ 98 St. George
☐ 24 Healy	☐ 55 Ladame	☐ 78 Oliver	☐ 99 Camp

$1.75 each

☐ 100 Stanford	☐ 104 Vitek	☐ 108 Hampson	☐ 112 Stanford
☐ 101 Hardy	☐ 105 Eden	☐ 109 Vernon	☐ 113 Browning
☐ 102 Hastings	☐ 106 Dailey	☐ 110 Trent	☐ 114 Michaels
☐ 103 Cork	☐ 107 Bright	☐ 111 South	☐ 115 John
	☐ 116 Lindley	☐ 117 Scott	

Introducing
First Love from
Silhouette

Romances for teenage girls to build their dreams on.

They're wholesome, fulfilling, supportive novels about every young girl's dreams. Filled with the challenges, excitement— and responsibilities—of love's first blush, *First Love* paperbacks prepare young adults to stand at the threshold of maturity with confidence and composure.

Introduce your daughter, or some young friend to the *First Love* series by giving her a one-year subscription to these romantic originals, written by leading authors. She'll receive two NEW $1.75 romances each month, a total of 24 books a year. Send in your coupon now. **There's nothing quite as special as a First Love.**

15-Day Free Trial Offer
6 Silhouette Romances

6 Silhouette Romances, free for 15 days! We'll send you 6 new Silhouette Romances to keep for 15 days, absolutely free! If you decide not to keep them, send them back to us. You pay nothing.

Free Home Delivery. But if you enjoy them as much as we think you will, keep them by paying the invoice enclosed with your free trial shipment. We'll pay all shipping and handling charges. You get the convenience of Home Delivery and we pay the postage and handling charge each month.

Don't miss a copy. The Silhouette Book Club is the way to make sure you'll be able to receive every new romance we publish before they're sold out. There is no minimum number of books to buy and you can cancel at any time.

This offer expires June 30, 1982